Watch Me
By Shelley Bradley

To stop a blackmailer and achieve her dreams, she only had to do one thing: seduce the enemy.

Shanna York was set to achieve her glittering ballroom dreams and become a dance champion—until her dance partner gets tangled up in scandal and blackmail. With the clock ticking and all her ambitions at stake, the last thing she needs is the gorgeous owner of a sex club tempting her with the forbidden.

Or maybe that's the very thing she needs...

Alejandro Diaz has sizzled for Shanna since he set eyes on her months ago. Her repeated rebuffs will make her surrender that much sweeter. She's ambitious and driven...but so is he. When she asks for his assistance to ensnare a voyeuristic blackmailer with a video fetish, he doesn't hesitate to help her stage a bedroom trap. But neither is prepared to face scorching, endless passion, the blackmailer's real identity—or the undeniable love that grows between them.

Warning, this title contains the following: explicit sex, graphic language, ménage a trois.

Show Me
By Jaci Burton

He promises to indulge her secret fantasies, if only she dares to accept.

Socialite Janine Bartolino has always been in the public eye. Managing her late father's philanthropic interests, she keeps her pastimes above reproach. But when a surprise thirtieth birthday celebration at a private club opens her eyes to wicked pleasures, and an intriguing man offers her the chance of a lifetime to indulge her every secret fantasy, Janine takes a leap of faith...at great personal risk.

Phillipe "Del" Delacroix knows what Janine wants, even if she isn't aware of it herself—a chance to explore the world of voyeurs and exhibitionists. Soon, the once staid and reserved woman transforms into a daring and passionate lover, giving Del everything he could ask for in a partner. But when something happens that puts Janine's reputation, her career, all she's worked for, in jeopardy...Del must prove that loving him is worth the risk.

Warning, this title contains the following: explicit sex, graphic language and woooo hooooo!!!—sex in public places!

Sneak Peek

A Samhain Publishing, Ltd. publication.

Samhain Publishing, Ltd.
577 Mulberry Street, Suite 1520
Macon, GA 31201
www.samhainpublishing.com

Sneak Peek
Watch Me Copyright © 2009 by Shelley Bradley
Show Me Copyright © 2009 by Jaci Burton
Print ISBN: 978-1-60504-094-3

Editing by Angela James
Cover by Scott Carpenter

Watch Me, ISBN 1-59998-525-X
First Samhain Publishing, Ltd. electronic publication: July 2007
Show Me, ISBN 1-59998-526-8
First Samhain Publishing, Ltd. electronic publication: July 2007
First Samhain Publishing, Ltd. print publication: January 2009

Contents

Watch Me

Shelley Bradley

Chapter One

Who'd have known it would only take two minutes, seventeen seconds to ruin her life?

Shanna York popped the DVD out of her laptop, resisting the childish urge to fling it across the room and watch it smash into a thousand pieces. Instead, she set it gently on the table beside her and stood.

Damn Kristoff! What *had* he been thinking?

Besides looking for inventive ways to get off, absolutely nothing. That was obvious.

Life as she'd wished it to be was over. Goodbye, California Dance Star competition, which she and Kristoff were favored to win in just over two weeks. *Adios*, any chance of making World Cup Latin finals—something she'd been working to attain her entire dance career.

Kristoff knew how important this season was to her. *Knew* it. She was twenty-eight—old by ballroom standards. He was the best partner she'd ever had, which was saying something. This year was their year; everyone said so.

All it had taken was one round disc recorded just last week, according to the date in the lower right corner of the screen, and a note with a scrawled "Watch me" to shatter her dreams.

Sighing, Shanna closed her eyes and tried to think. But that only brought every image on the DVD to full, Technicolor memory. Kristoff, tall and ungodly handsome, standing above two figures, one male, the other female. He cradled each of their heads in his hands as they knelt before him. Their tongues slid up and down his erection, licked over his balls, and occasionally met at the head of his cock for a juicy kiss.

"You like that big dick?" he asked them. They both moaned. The camera zoomed in as the woman, a stunning blonde with a starburst tattoo on her breast, deep-throated Kristoff.

The other male, a buff guy with military short hair and his own raging hard-on, stood and licked at Kristoff's nipples. Kristoff groaned, the sound soon drowned out by the man capturing his lips and devouring them in a harsh kiss.

That was the first thirty seconds—plenty depraved by the traditional standards many ballroom judges held. Then came the middle of the clip...

Kristoff intent and focused as he penetrated the woman's sex, plunging in for slow, agonizing strokes. A surprise, given the fact Shanna had always believed he was gay. But thrusting into the woman, he appeared like any other hetero man...until the camera panned back and showed the other man penetrating Kristoff's ass, the forward momentum of that stroke pushing Kristoff's erection into the panting woman.

The end of the DVD, however, was what Shanna knew really killed her dreams of being a ballroom champion. The other man, apparently at the end of his restraint, tore off his condom and stood near the woman's sex as Kristoff so diligently pounded it. The dark-haired man watched them, yanking on his cock until semen shot out, coating the woman's clit and wet folds. They all groaned.

Kristoff quickly pulled out of her, tugged on his erection,

and came on the woman's swollen sex, too. She dripped semen, oozed with the fluids of the men's satisfaction. Was that enough for Kristoff? Of course not.

He grabbed the other man's shoulders and forced him to kneel before the woman's dripping sex beside him. Together, they licked her. Clean. Deep. Until she orgasmed against their dueling tongues. During the clip's final moments, the camera panned back again to reveal the fact the trio had performed all of this for an audience.

Shanna put her head in her hands and groaned. She was so screwed. If the conservative judges of ever-elegant ballroom dance got hold of this DVD... The thought of what they could—and would—do to her and Kristoff's scores at the California Dance Star made her shudder. Nothing like going from first to worst in the standings.

Even worse, as if her life wasn't messed up enough, was the fact that watching the scene had been vaguely arousing. Not that she was attracted to Kristoff—and definitely not after this stunt. But the freedom to just let loose and have wild sex, even with people watching...

Damn, she had to get hold of herself!

Where was that ass, Kristoff? He had to have known that his recent jaunts to that damn sex club, Sneak Peek, would eventually come back to haunt them. She'd warned him. Clearly, he hadn't heeded a word.

The door burst open into her small dressing room. Kristoff glided, graceful bastard. Like glass on the dance floor, which had been a treat after living with an Olympic sprinter, a world-class decathlete, a former champion weightlifter, and a pro football player. Her father and brothers, all of whom considered her a failure because she'd never been a champion. By their definition, ballroom dancing wasn't even a sport. Which made her a double loser.

This year, she'd intended to show them different.

With Kristoff's one night at that crazy sex club for exhibitionists and voyeurs, her dreams were gone.

"Three minutes, Shan. Are you ready?" From the doorway, Kristoff held out his hand to her.

Normally, that was Shanna's cue to take it and follow his lead. Not tonight.

"You goddamn idiot!" She held up the DVD. "Do you have a brain, or did it sink into your pants? Could you not have waited to get your jollies for another few weeks?"

He frowned, looking totally unamused. "What are you talking about?"

"You went to Sneak Peek and got yourself into a threesome."

Kristoff's polished smile faded. "I was just, um, how do you say, blowing off a little steam. How did you know?"

"Someone filmed you, moron, and sent me the DVD. Full color, high quality, great sound, no question it's you near a sign that said Sneak Peek."

"Filmed me... I had no idea. And someone sent it to you?" he croaked. "You saw it?"

"Yes, along with a little note informing me that if we show up to the California Star, they'll distribute the clip to all the judges. And you know what will happen if they do. We'll have no chance in hell of winning."

He cursed a popular Angelo-Saxon syllable that started with an F. Shanna shook her head. He'd already done that, thanks so much.

"I agreed to take you as my partner for two reasons: You're a hell of a dancer, and I thought you were discreetly gay. Gay, the judges can handle. Discreetly gay, even better. Clearly, I was wrong about your orientation, so your talent no longer matters."

Kristoff flushed. "I am, um, equal opportunity when it comes to sex."

"I gathered that from this Oscar-winning material." She gritted her teeth.

"One minute!" someone shouted from the hall.

Squatting, Shanna peered into the mirror at her dressing table, secured a pin holding a lock of her pale blonde hair in place, then smoothed a hand down the silver sequins of her tiny costume. God, she felt sick to her stomach. All the years of sacrifice and work... If she wanted to win—and she did—she was probably going to have to start over. New season...new partner. Damn it! She hoped her tumult didn't show on her face.

"We have to go," she said. "Or we'll be late."

"Stop! We have things to talk about. Winning is important to me, too, and—"

"Champions aren't late."

"Why do you care? This is a charity event, not a competition, and I bet your dance card is empty."

Ouch! Still, she lifted her chin, despite his low blow. "Not the point. People are still watching."

"Not everything is work. Must you be so driven? Enjoy life a little!"

"I enjoy winning." Her teeth hurt from grinding them together.

"Except for dance, you have no life. When did you last go on a date?"

"Are you keeping track?"

"I grow tired of your so-serious attitude. Maybe you need to go to Sneak Peek and um, how do you say, let loose like me."

"We have the biggest competition of our careers in three weeks, and you think I need to get laid?"

"Yes."

Shanna tried not to see red. And violet. And crimson. And magenta.

Kristoff met her angry gaze squarely. "Until you smile and be nice, you are not fun to work with. You will certainly make no money for the cause tonight in this mood."

It might be uncharitable of her, but it was hard to think about someone else's cause when her own was falling apart.

"Go to hell, Mr. Palavin!" She made to stalk past him.

He grabbed her arm to stay her. "You are angry. I fucked up, yes. I am sorry. Very sorry. I know what this means to you. But no matter how much I apologize, no matter that we have become friends in the past year, will you forgive me? Stand by me? By tomorrow, I believe you will be holding auditions, because everyone knows any partner who is a liability to your ambition is quickly replaced." He grabbed the DVD off the table. "There is a reason your dance card is empty tonight and everyone calls you the Bitch of the Ballroom. In the past, I have defended you, but now... Have a lovely time alone."

"Are you staring at that *ramera* again?"

Alejandro Diaz ripped his gaze away from Shanna York and sent a rebuking stare to his dance partner. "*Mamá*, you've been listening to gossip. We do not know her well enough to know if she's a bitch."

But he'd looked at her enough to know he wanted her. Bad.

Her soft blonde hair shone under the lights like a halo around her face. Those blue, blue eyes projected a little-girl-lost quality that made him want to hold her close and whisper reassurances. But the fiery way she moved her killer body when she danced, like she performed sex to music, made him hard as hell.

Oh, the fantasies he had about her, about taking her to Sneak Peek and melting away all that icy reserve by stripping her down, tying her up, filling her full of his cock...all while wondering if they were being watched. And she'd wonder—if others could see the rise of her pleasure, hear the gasps of her orgasms as he gave them to her, one after the other. The way Shanna danced lured men in, as if she loved having their eyes on her, as if she craved hot stares and even hotter thoughts of strangers.

Yes, he had *lots* of fantasies about her.

His mother shook her head. "Hmm. You met her once. She was not polite."

Not true. She'd been polite, in an icy, stand-offish way. In retrospect he'd come on too strong. Been too direct. Clearly not the way to approach a strong woman who valued being in control.

"Tonight is another night." He turned his mother around the dance floor in a gentle waltz.

And he watched Shanna. Her appearance lived up to her ice princess reputation in a short, silvery, barely-there costume of sequins and crystals. She was stiff, unsmiling, aloof. He'd love to melt her.

"There are other young, single girls here. Girls who are good. And Catholic. And yet you focus on the *ramera rubia*."

"*Mamá*," Alejandro warned. "Just because she's blonde, does not make her guilty of being a bitch."

He sighed. He loved his mother and owed her so much. As a single woman, she'd raised him with loving arms and a firm hand, since his father had left them just before Alejandro became a teenager. She hadn't given him much in the way of luxuries as a kid, but she'd made up for it by providing all the affection and guidance he'd needed. As an adult, however, he realized she was incredibly old-fashioned.

"Spending too much time at that club of yours has confused your thinking, *mijo*. Nothing but *putas* there."

Alejandro laughed. His mother didn't disapprove of the club...but she only knew about the bar and pool tables, the dart boards and the dance floor. She had no idea what went on upstairs.... Better to keep it that way.

He made damn good money as Sneak Peek's co-owner. Between that, his other stash of money, and his investments, he'd been able to buy his mother a condo and a new car, set up a trust for her, and give her a bit of luxury in the last two years. She just wanted him to settle down, marry, have babies. *Mamá* had made that *very* clear.

He would...in his own good time.

"Let's not argue." He twirled her toward the punch table, not far from where Shanna sat alone. As he looked at the gorgeous dancer again, he had to fight the rise of his erection. Not here, not now...but soon.

His mother followed the line of his sight. "*Dios mío*, can you not look at one other woman tonight?"

No. He'd come tonight specifically to cozy up to Shanna York. What a happy coincidence that making his mother's night would help him to make his own.

"*Mamá*, did you sign up to dance with your favorites tonight?"

She shook her head. "No."

"Why not?"

"Alejandro, it is too much money. You paid for me to be here, and that is enough. I will watch."

And send a disapproving stare every time he rumbaed Shanna into a dark corner? Not a chance.

"You will dance."

He stopped her before the punch table and handed her a drink. While she sipped, he eased over to the table that held the dancers' cards. There were still a few empty slots available to foxtrot or tango with some of her favorites. And Shanna's card was completely empty. He smiled and wrote his mother's name onto the empty spaces of the male dancers' cards, wrote his own on Shanna's in every space, and called the attendant over.

After settling dances for his mother, he handed the volunteer, a perky brunette, Shanna's card. "I would like to purchase all the dances, as well."

The brunette looked at it and frowned. "Hers? All of them?"

"*Sí.*"

"That's three thousand dollars."

He smiled as he handed her his credit card. "Then I will have the pleasure of knowing more children will have full bellies and be attending school, while I dance with a beautiful woman."

The woman sent him a look that plainly said she thought he was unhinged. "She isn't known for keeping her partners long. You may not last the whole night."

Wrong. But for what he had in mind, a night was all he needed.

With a smile, he finished paying, then found his mother.

"The charity dances start in five minutes, and you will be busy." He handed her a schedule of her partners.

"Alejandro! You spend too much money on an old woman. I

17

cannot dance so much."

"*Mamá*, you are barely fifty. It's only money, and I can afford it. Enjoy yourself."

He certainly planned to.

Chapter Two

The event's emcee announced the beginning of the charity dances, and Shanna poised herself in a chair, plastic smile in place, at the edge of the ballroom floor.

People around her were beginning to pair up for the first of the dances, names and smiles being exchanged. She tossed her hair off her shoulders. That twisting of her stomach was not a pang of hurt. She didn't care if no one bid on her dances. Sitting back would give her an opportunity to observe her competition, since most of the other dancers were here...just in case she and Kristoff somehow won, in spite of his indiscreet sex life.

Tomorrow, she'd find some way to destroy or discredit that shocking DVD. She wasn't giving up on years of hard work and her dreams of being a champion without a fight.

"I believe this dance is mine."

Shanna followed the deep voice and looked up into an incredibly handsome face. Strong features, burning hazel eyes, heavy five-o'clock shadow, perfectly tailored gray suit with a vavoom red tie. Her heart lurched; this one had sin written all over him.

He also looked familiar. She stared, hesitating, but the more she thought about it, the more certain she became. Somewhere, somehow, they'd crossed paths before.

"Have we met?"

He smiled, all dazzling charm, oozing Latin charisma and hot sex. "Yes. Three months ago. The Bartolino Foundation thing."

That night rushed back to her with overwhelming clarity. This sexy man with his killer smile flirting outrageously and whispering shocking, hot suggestions as he tangoed her around the dance floor. At the end of the night, he'd asked her out...while trying to kiss her. She'd been incredibly tempted—and that was saying something for a woman who'd easily refused every man for nearly two years. But this man might as well have the word *distraction* tattooed on his forehead. Go out with him? No way, no how. She'd refused him and disappeared into the crowd. She assumed she'd seen the last of him.

Somehow, she got the feeling she'd underestimated him.

"Ah, I think you recall that night." A smile lifted the edges of his lips.

"Alejandro, isn't it?"

"Alejandro Diaz, yes."

Shanna drew in a deep breath. Just like their first meeting, he caused an unwelcome dizzying effect, complete with revving heartbeat. *Warning!* When she dated, which was rarely, she chose safe men—guys who were rich, too busy with their own careers to be demanding, and far too dull to keep her interest for more than an evening. She just didn't have time for a relationship when she had a dance career that needed all her time and attention.

This one might as well shout that he'd be both fascinating and determined. He *would* get his way—and have his way with her.

Not if she could help it.

Steeling herself against the impact of his touch, Shanna put her hand in his. No matter how prepared she thought she'd been for the skin-on-skin contact, she'd been wrong. A wild gong of want beat through her the second her palm brushed his. She braced for the rush of heat as she rose to her feet.

"The music is starting. Shall we?" He gestured to the dance floor, then eased her forward with a hand at the small of her back.

"Sure." What else could she say? This was his three minutes; he'd paid for them, so she owed him that. But no more.

God, not a second more.

A soft Latin rhythm began to wash through the room from the overhead speakers. Sensual, hypnotic, the music spoke of a humid summer night shared by lovers. Shanna nearly groaned. Great, a rumba, the dance of love. The one that most emulated passion and sex. Why now?

On a strong beat, Alejandro grabbed her wrist and pulled her against him. Shanna tried to stop herself from crashing into him by planting a hand on his chest. But her fingers only encountered hard muscle. Oh God, he was like a rock under that shirt, and given his mile-wide shoulders, she was suddenly sure that seeing him naked would be ten times better than a slice of her favorite sinful chocolate cake.

He hooked a finger under her chin. Reluctantly, she lifted her gaze to his. The heat in those hazel eyes fired molten gold. *Look away. Get away!* But she couldn't. Once her gaze connected with his, she was locked in, fused to him in a way she didn't understand. And didn't like.

That stare sizzled all through her...and settled right between her legs. She blinked, unable to break his gaze.

Sex had always been something she could take or leave. At

the moment, she wanted to take anything he was willing to dish out.

How could he do that with just a glance?

As she drew in a deep breath and tried to find her wits, he curled a thick arm around her waist, drawing her even closer. His whole body was hard...every inch of it. From the feel of him, many inches. Shanna trembled to realize his body was every bit as interested as hers was. Thank God these dances were short.

Then he held out his left hand, palm up. Slowly, she placed her hand in his.

They began to dance. He was incredibly smooth, never dancing on his heels, never losing the beat of the music. Wow, could he move his hips. Perfect figure eights with them. No doubt, he'd learned how to dance very well somewhere along the way.

Basic boxes quickly gave way to an open position, then a cross, which he used as an opportunity to brush his body against hers and caress her hip. An underarm turn led her right back to a basic.

Oh, this guy was good for an amateur. She had an inkling that he might be good at...other things.

"So, what brings you here tonight?" she asked, grasping at conversational straws. Maybe if she was talking, she wouldn't be thinking about how much this guy turned her on.

"Helping orphans is not a worthwhile cause?"

"It is. Most men would rather simply write a check than ballroom dance."

"I brought my mother. She enjoys these things, and it is a very small thing to do in order to see her smile."

Sexy, a good dancer, family-oriented, crazy handsome, Alejandro seemed like every woman's fantasy. He had to be too good to be true, have some terrible flaw she just couldn't see at the moment. If not...Lord, she was in a lot of trouble.

Her body temperature rose with every suggestive look, every sweep of his hand over her waist and low dive on her hip, each brush of his palm that inched toward her ass.

Damn! Why hadn't she found some man to scratch her itch in the last two years? Or even invested in a good vibrator? Maybe if she had, she wouldn't feel wound so tightly right now, so ready to jump on Alejandro and every protruding part of his body.

"That's nice of you," she managed to say.

"Not really. I knew you would be here."

"M—me?"

"Hmm." He led her into another open position, then curled her against his body, hips crushed against hips. And she felt more than his pelvis. Way more.

"Certainly you can feel my...enthusiasm to meet you again." He laughed, seemingly at himself.

Yeah. His enthusiasm was sizeable and very hard to miss.

Then he leaned her back over his arm in an exaggerated dip and followed her down. Until his face was an inch from her breasts. Shanna felt him exhale, his warm breath on her cleavage. Her nipples beaded instantly.

Slowly, he lifted her back upright, then spun her around, until her back rested against his chest. And he nestled his erection in the small of her back. The flat of his palm covered her abdomen, and he took her other hand in his. The gesture probably looked proprietary. It certainly felt that way.

Straight ahead, she saw Kristoff dancing with a thin, middle-aged woman with hair a dubious shade of red. He peered at her with a questioning brow raised.

Alejandro led her to swivel her hips against his, in time with the music. Kristoff didn't miss a second of it. In fact, as Shanna looked around, she realized they'd gathered quite a bit of attention.

A blast of moisture flooded her thong.

"Everyone is watching," he whispered.

"Yes." Her voice shook.

He bent and lifted her leg, wrapping her calf around his thigh and urging her head to fall back to his shoulder. Their eyes met, their mouths inches apart.

Shanna felt stripped down, as if she were naked under Alejandro's knowing gaze. God, if he didn't stop that, she'd melt against him in seconds.

"Men are watching you, wanting you."

He grabbed her thigh, spun her around to face him, then placed that thigh over his hip. They rested nearly hip to hip again. As he leaned back slightly, he forced her chest against his. Still, she could not break his stare.

"You like it," he whispered.

She opened her mouth to deny it, but Alejandro's gaze stopped her, warning her before she could do anything foolish, like lie.

"I know you do."

The intensity of his stare, the way in which he'd dug past her icy defenses, seemed to see the real her, and guessed her dirty secret... He was a walking wet dream.

He was her worst nightmare.

He swayed with the music in the opposite direction, bringing her body with him. With a gentle caress of her cheek, he directed her gaze back to his—all while making it look like a part of the dance.

"You know you do," he murmured. "You love knowing that most every man in the room right now would kill to have your body against his and have a front-row seat of that smoldering sensuality you keep wrapped in ice suddenly melting in a pool at his feet."

His words made her shake. *Oh, no. No!* "Stop."

He performed an open step, then brought her back for a box. "Their eyes cling to you as you lure them in with the sway of your hips to the music and your femininity. Their gazes caress your breasts as your chest lifts with every move and breath. They watch the sleek movements of those gorgeous thighs and wish they were between them."

A glance around proved he was totally right. Easily a dozen men were openly watching her and Alejandro dance, their gazes ranging from more than mildly interested to sizzling with heat. Desire vibrated deep inside her, pulsing under her clit. How wet could she get before it stained the front of her thin costume?

And how had Alejandro known what turned her on?

Most people had only seen the driven dancer who yearned to win and find some way to make her family proud. No one else had seen the woman inside who used dance to express the sexuality she otherwise repressed. No one.

This man had seen her hidden sensuality in the blink of an eye. He'd all but mocked her icy reserve. He looked at her as if he could see past it, all the way to the fear and emptiness that fed her ambition.

Thankfully, the music ended.

"Thank you for an interesting evening, Mr. Diaz. Perhaps our paths will cross again." Not if she could help it.

Still, he didn't let go, continued to stare at her with that sultry hint of a smile as the music began again. "The evening is not over. I bought all of your dances tonight, for the whole night."

Shanna stared at him, wide eyed and stunned. Panicked. He'd bought *all* of her dances? She swallowed. That was bad. Very bad. Just being in his arms and hearing his words made her feel vulnerable in a way she didn't like and would not accept.

And she was stuck with him for the next three hours? Lord, she was in so much trouble.

"Why?"

"I enjoy watching you being watched and the way it arouses you. I love knowing that so many men in the room are fantasizing about slaking their lust with you—"

"You can't know what other men are thinking," she protested.

"But I can. It is exactly what I'm thinking. It is even more delicious because I alone am holding you in my arms."

Oh, God. Oh, God. "This conversation is inappropriate."

"Honesty disturbs you?"

"I'm not...I—I don't get aroused knowing that men are watching me."

"Really?"

He urged her into a cross again. No sooner than she turned to step into the next box, he pushed against her hand, sending her spinning to face the wall. Then he was behind her, hands on her swaying hips, his mouth hovering just over her sensitive neck in a darkened corner of the ballroom.

Shanna shivered as he exhaled, quivered as he gripped her hips.

Then he reached around to place his hand flat on her stomach again...but he aimed high, flattening his palm on the upper swells of her chest and smoothing his way down.

"Hard nipples," he commented. "Little edible, want-to-suck-them-in-my-mouth nipples."

She hissed in a breath, and opened her mouth to stop him, tell him to get lost...but he kept tantalizing her as he caressed his way south, down her ribs, over her stomach, until his fingers brushed the front of her costume right over her sex. He lingered. Shame and arousal crashed inside her. She closed her eyes. Her thong was about to overflow.

"You're always wet when you dance in public...like now, aren't you?"

At his touch, his words, pleasure spiked, hitting her full force, like a blast from a raging fire. She sucked in a breath. Damn it, why did he have to be right?

If he could figure that much out after just a few minutes with her, Shanna knew he'd dig deeper, quickly, into her soul, unless she put distance between them now.

"Stop," she demanded in her best ice-queen voice.

"Answer me, *querida*."

"No."

He danced her to face him again as one song segued into the next, this one a waltz.

"Do not be embarrassed. Your arousal turns me on. It's one of the reasons I chose not to give up when you rebuffed me at the Bartolino event. I want that arousal," he whispered in her ear, making her shiver. "I want it in my hands, my mouth, all around my cock when I fuck you and you wonder exactly who is watching us."

His words hit her like lava, sizzling her skin, charring her resistance and sanity. No one had ever talked to her like that. Between her brothers and the bitchiness she wore like armor, no one had dared.

God, even without uttering a word, Alejandro was stunning. When he talked like that, he didn't just turn her on; he turned her inside out.

Alejandro was dangerous to her career and her focus. She could see getting lost in such a man and the smoldering promise of spectacular sex—which she'd never experienced—in his hazel eyes.

"That's enough," she forced herself to say.

"We haven't started. I think about undressing you under soft lights, your back to my front and letting my hand smooth your dress from your lush curves. I ache to let your perfect hard nipples brush the inside of my palms before I roll them between my fingers. I fantasize about feeling my way lower, down to that soft, wet pussy, and grazing your hard clit. And stroking it until you come. I obsess about bending you over and filling you with my cock—all while you know hot eyes, strangers' eyes, touch you."

Desire pulsed, flared with every mental image he created. She could *see* herself naked, flushed, writhing under his hands or as he impaled her. She could feel herself dissolving at the thought of orgasming for him—and a roomful of aroused men.

This was dangerous. Bad. Wrong. *No, no, no.*

"I said that's enough!" Her voice shook as hard as the rest of her.

He kept on, as if she'd never uttered a protest. "I am part owner of a club where you could express yourself in any way you like. In every way that gets you off. Sneak Peek was made for women like you."

Sneak Peek? That jolted her. The club where Kristoff's video had been filmed in his soon-to-be-infamous threesome? The very one.

"I know what goes on there."

A smile toyed with those sensual lips of his. "Good. If we weren't waltzing, I would reach down between those sweet thighs of yours, and I bet I would find out you're even wetter now than the last time I touched you."

Shanna started to lie, tell him it wasn't true. She didn't trust him not to waltz her in a corner and test his theory, now that he knew her body didn't care about being discreet, just about being wild—and watched.

"I need to use the ladies' room."

He hesitated, then released her. "By all means."

She turned away, resisting the urge to run to the sanctuary of her dressing room. No, she would walk. Calmly. *Breathe in, breathe out.*

And screw charity. Alejandro had paid his money and gotten his dance—and his cheap feel. He could pat himself on the back, knowing that he'd dug up her naughty secret and rubbed it in her face. She wasn't coming back, and he could deal with it. If she ever saw him at one of these charity events again, she'd run in the other direction. Fast.

Before she could take the first step, he grabbed her wrist and pulled her back. Suddenly off balance, she collided against his chest. Her head snapped back...her mouth right under his.

"At Sneak Peek, I will fulfill your every fantasy."

Of that, she had no doubt. But she wasn't going to give him that chance.

Chapter Three

"So I've got two choices, both really lousy." Shanna sighed as she stirred her hot tea at the outdoor café's wrought iron table the next morning. "Either I stick it out and hope this threat is just a sick joke or I dump Kristoff, try to find yet another new partner, and wait a season or two before we mesh well enough to win anything."

Jonathan winced. "Don't you think it's time you stop dropping partners, love? Your reputation in that area isn't exactly sparkling."

With a frosty glare, she reminded her former dance partner, "Ending our partnership was a mutual decision."

The handsome Aussie reached for her hand across the table. "The handwriting was on the wall. We weren't going to make it. I didn't want to win as badly as you did. And sleeping together was a terrible mistake."

Shanna wanted to deny his assertion, but couldn't. Jonathan simply hadn't possessed her drive to win. They'd both known it. Their one night of impulsive sex had merely brought their problems to the fore.

Admittedly, sex between them had been stupid. But a late-night practice, Jonathan suffering a recent break-up with his fiancée, Shanna fearing their days of competing together were numbered, hours upon hours of nothing but sexually charged dances, with the tension between them so thick... The dam holding their restraint had burst.

Afterward, their partnership had gone from strained to doomed. Her ambition on the dance floor hadn't meshed well with his need to check out to deal with his anguish and confusion. Shanna had realized he needed more emotional support from a partner than she'd been able to give. Their fights became hellacious. They'd said terrible things, and he'd walked out.

In retrospect, the end of their dance partnership had been best for both of them. Jonathan's fiancée had returned, and he'd retired to married life and modeling. After a few months of silence between them, he'd reached out to her. Over the last eighteen months, they'd repaired their friendship. During that time, Shanna had been happily paired with Kristoff...until she'd seen his porn-inspired DVD.

"Let's not rehash ancient history," Jonathan said. "You came to me with a problem. Are you sleeping with Kristoff?"

Shanna recoiled. "Absolutely not! Until I saw the video, I thought he was firmly in the gay column."

"At least that's one less complication."

The early morning breeze whipped through her hair. Shanna looked down into her steaming mug and nodded. "I have to decide what to do. I don't want to lose Kristoff as a partner. Training a new one would take so much damn time. But if the judges get their hands on that DVD..."

"That would be devastating. The old crones would crucify you. The men...they'd either try to bury or debauch you."

"Exactly. I want to strangle Kristoff every time I think about what he's done. He's jeopardized everything, the stupid ass."

"In the dance department, you're well-matched. Kristoff is a fabulous athlete who wants to win just as badly as you do.

Admit that much."

She rolled her eyes. "I suppose."

"Stop." He demanded. "I know you too well. Everyone else may buy that puffed-up bitch act, but we both know better. It took me years to realize you're not half as pissed as you are afraid. You're trembling at the thought of being vulnerable and of not holding that trophy so you can finally prove to your family that you're a champion. Is Daddy's opinion really more important than friendship? It's okay to stand by your friends, even if your family will disapprove."

God, he had her number. And she hated that.

"Have you taken up psychotherapy on the side, Freud?"

"Just calling your bluff."

"No, I came to you for help, and you're giving me hell." She stood and grabbed her paper mug.

"Sorry," Jonathan murmured, looking like he wanted to say more on the subject. Mercifully, he didn't. "Do you have any other information about the tape or its delivery that might help you track down the blackmailer? Or did Kristoff know anything about how it was made?"

"No, I don't think Kristoff has a clue. But last night, the owner of the sex club in which the footage was filmed tried to seduce me out of my panties. If the event hadn't been for charity—"

"You know where this tape was made?"

She nodded. "A place called Sneak Peek."

"The club for voyeurs and exhibitionists?"

He knew about that place? "Yes."

Jonathan sat back in his chair, a taunting smile curling up his mouth. Shanna felt her heart seize. He looked at her as if he knew being watched made her wet. Did he? Did every man who watched her dance? She swallowed, horrified...and incredibly aroused.

Thankfully, he didn't go there. "So when you danced with this bloke, did you talk to him, see what he knows about the tape and its creation?"

"No." She'd been too busy resisting his seduction, trying to fend off his unnerving ability to see past her defenses.

"There you go." He shrugged. "Maybe he can help you track down who's blackmailing Kristoff."

Shanna gripped her tea. Jonathan was right. The answer had been staring her in the face. Alejandro could find out exactly who had filmed Kristoff.

All she had to do was put herself in his path again.

God help her.

"I need your help."

Alejandro Diaz looked up at the trembling female voice. Platinum hair pulled tightly away from a pale face. Blue eyes smudged with the bruises of sleeplessness. Shanna York. Here, in his office.

Well, didn't this make his morning interesting?

"Long trip to the ladies' room," he drawled.

She tossed her head, lifting her chin—her silent way of telling him she would not bend her pride to apologize for having deserted him last night. Alejandro frowned...though he was silently amused.

"You came on too strong. Again. I needed to put space between us."

"And now you do not? Today, I am supposed to forget that I

enjoyed a mere two and a half dances, rather than the eight I paid for."

"You gave that money to charity."

"To be with you. The charity was the cherry on top."

"You paid for the opportunity to dance with me, not seduce me."

Why not both? he wanted to ask, but tactically retreated from that line of questioning. Starting a fight with her wasn't the way to entice her to stay. Putting up her defenses would not get him what he wanted—up close and very personal time with her.

"Perhaps I succeeded, since you have come to Sneak Peek saying you need me."

"No. I'd still be avoiding you if I didn't need your help." She swallowed. "Which I need now. Please."

Hmm. She'd likely choked on that word. Shanna was stubborn and tough and wore her ice like armor. No doubt it warded off most men.

He was made of stronger stuff.

Alejandro stood and faced her. "What can I do for you? Take you on a tour? We have great facilities."

Her expression softened. "It's a beautiful place. I was expecting something…"

"Dark? Sleazy? Dirty?"

She hesitated. "Glass-and-chrome seedy. This is really…warm."

That's what had attracted him to the house in the beginning. Alejandro thanked God every time he set foot in the place that his business partner, Del, had agreed with his choice of location. Its shimmering white plaster walls glowed Hollywood golden when the sun set over the hills of Los

Angeles. The expansive gardens had a charming Spanish Revival feel, complete with decorative tile that rimmed the pool and outlined the patio steps leading to the second floor. The bars both indoors and outdoors welcomed guests. Converting the house into a club had given it the feel of an intimate party, rather than a bunch of strangers getting naked together. That instant comfort level was one of the reasons he and Del had been so successful since opening Sneak Peek. That and good business sense.

Alejandro shrugged. "I took one look at the house and fell in love. Cary Grant built it in the 1920s. The previous owners started restoring it about ten years ago...and ran out of money. Del and I spent a small fortune to buy the place and finish fixing it up. I have not regretted it."

"It's gorgeous."

"As are you. Since it's clear you are not here for me to seduce, what can I do for you?"

Her charmed smile disappeared. The tense hand-clasping returned. "My dance partner and I have a...situation. A delicate one. Kristoff has been here, as a customer, right?"

"I'm not at liberty to answer that. Privacy is something we protect fiercely here at Sneak Peek. I hope you understand."

"But that's just it. Someone invaded his privacy. They filmed him..." She shook her head. "It would be better if I showed you."

Alejandro frowned as Shanna reached into an oversized bag hanging from her shoulder and extracted a DVD in a clear plastic case. She handed it to him with a tense expression. He popped it into his laptop.

Two and a half minutes later, his blood was boiling—more from anger than any arousal.

"Where did you get this?"

"Someone left it in my dressing room last night just before the benefit began, along with a note telling me that if we competed in the upcoming California Dance Star, this DVD will be sent to all the judges."

"And neither you nor Kristoff have any idea who sent this?"

She shook her head. "That's why I'm here. I was hoping you could help me. That competition means...everything to me. I've worked *years* to win this."

As driven as she was, as ambitious as rumor painted her, Alejandro believed it. She had dumped three partners in the last five years. One after breaking his leg badly skiing just before dance season began. The next partner had been history when he dropped her during a lift—in the middle of a competition. The third...he was a mystery. There one day, gone the next. Alejandro's mother had the pulse on all her favorite and not-so-favorite dancers. *Mamá* said there had been rumors of a torrid affair between Shanna and Jonathan Smythe.

Alejandro extracted the DVD, slotted it back in its case, and handed it to her. "There are absolutely no still or video cameras allowed in the club. Period. That is part of our strict privacy policy."

"Which someone clearly violated."

"Yes, because that isn't security footage. If it was, it would be black and white and from an aerial view. It certainly wouldn't be in full color and focused in tight on the action." Alejandro rose, paced.

This was very bad news. People paid a lot of money to enjoy themselves at the club anonymously. Often high profile people. Stars, senators, diplomats. If that privacy was compromised and people found out... He didn't want to think about what it might do to their business.

"Would you excuse me?" he asked.

She hesitated, looking decidedly unhappy. "Yes."

Alejandro pulled his cell phone from the clip at his waistband and hit the speed dial button to reach his partner.

"Del?" he asked after hearing a familiar voice rumble at the other end. "We have a situation you ought to know about."

"I'll be there in five."

It was more like ten minutes later when Del sauntered in, buttoning his shirt and wearing a smile and mussed hair. Damn, it was barely past ten in the morning, but already his buddy had been getting busy. A glance at Shanna reminded him that he hadn't been busy like that in longer than he cared to admit...and he knew exactly who he would like to change that fact with.

"What's up, Ali?"

"Del, this is Shanna York. She is a professional ballroom dancer. Shanna, my business partner Del."

Shanna held out a prim little hand for a professional shake. Del, being the Frenchman he was, enveloped her hand and brought it to his mouth for a soft kiss. "*Enchanté.*"

No doubt he was enchanted, but this wasn't a free-for-all.

"Back off," Alejandro growled in Del's ear.

His friend sent him a dark-eyed look of annoyance. Alejandro shrugged. Del would get over it.

When Shanna snatched her hand away, Alejandro had to smile. Classic! When had any woman ever taken one look at Del and pulled back? Never. Usually, they threw themselves at his dark stubble, wealth, and bad attitude.

"This is Shanna's situation..."

Alejandro clued Del in, and Shanna provided the DVD for viewing again. After the clip ended, Del was gnashing his teeth and looking none too happy.

"I wish I knew who to beat the shit out of for violating the rules."

"Me, too," Alejandro agreed.

"Okay, so you don't know off the top of your heads who might have done it," Shanna said. "I'm assuming you know in which room this...event took place?"

"Yes," the men answered together.

"Maybe by figuring out who might have used the room in the last week, you can get a list of likely suspects. Do you keep records?"

"For payment purposes, yes," Del confirmed. "But that room, it's likely been used at least fifty times since that recording was made."

Shanna did the math. "Ten...events in there a *day*?"

With a shrug, Alejandro smiled. "We go through a lot of sheets."

Del laughed, the sound hearty and male.

"Oh, aren't you two cute. Freshman Frat Boy and his sidekick, Horny." She rolled her eyes. "I'm assuming you don't want it known that someone is sneaking into your club and recording your guests' most private actions without their consent or knowledge."

He and Del sobered up quickly. She was right. Business now. Pleasure...soon.

Still, his mind took a little detour. Her shock about the room's constant use was amusing, and it pleased him that she did not understand how addicting watching—and being watched—could be. Yet.

"Of course we don't want our guests compromised," Del cut in smoothly. "We could make a list of all the guests who have used this room in the last week, but I doubt it would help. In all honesty, I would never have believed any of our members would violate such a cardinal rule. The fee to join is steep enough to attract only serious members. The rules are absolute; there is no room for gray. We also have ways of ensuring that anyone who violates our rules finds themselves unwelcome at similar clubs in the state."

"This feels to me as if you were targeted specifically," Alejandro said. "The note was delivered to your dressing room, so close to a major competition..."

"That's it! Do any of my competitors belong to your club?"

Alejandro looked at Del, who looked back at him. That was the great thing about having been friends for nearly a decade. They could almost read each others' minds. Answering the question wasn't really giving away information...

"No. Just Kristoff. And he's recent. He came highly recommended, and has been very active since he joined."

"I'll bet." She snorted. "And here I thought he was your average, garden-variety gay man..."

Del choked. Alejandro resisted the urge to laugh himself.

Shanna swatted his shoulder. "Okay. I get from this DVD that's not true. You two can stop snickering now."

Alejandro couldn't resist her ruffled feathers for another second. He was dying to soothe them...right before he melted her.

"What about any of my former dance partners?" She directed the question to Alejandro. Not that she suspected Jonathan, but the first two hated her. "Do you know who they are?"

"No and yes. None of your former partners are members."

"Hmm." Shanna bit a pink, bee-stung lip as she thought. "Have any of your other members indicated this breach of privacy has been a problem for them?"

"Hell no! And we've established that the person who took the footage isn't one of your competitors, but it's clearly someone who knows something about your world of ballroom dance. About you and what you value."

"Yes," Del agreed. "Someone who knew that competition was coming up soon and that the judges would punish you if such a DVD was circulating. Someone who knew that competition was important to you."

"Any ideas who among your members that could be?" Shanna prompted.

Again, Alejandro looked at Del, who looked at him. "Not a clue. I could ask you the same question. Who are your enemies?"

Shanna's blue eyes darted around, as if scanning her memories. "No one else I can think of. If it's not a former partner or a competitor, I can't think of anyone who hates me enough to want to destroy me like this."

"Well, if any guest was a friend of one of your former partners or competitors, we have no way of knowing."

"True..." Shanna nibbled nervously on a hangnail, then, as if realizing she'd done something less than perfect, she stopped. "What about your employees? Any of them have access to video cameras and those rooms?"

Del shook his head. "We have four types of employees: security, maid service, wait staff and bartenders. That's it. They are paid to be invisible unless they're needed. None of those employees should be anywhere near a room when it's in use. All the watching and exhibiting is done for and with fellow members."

"So, another dead end..."

"It appears," Del agreed, then looked Alejandro's way. His buddy had the glint of the devil in his eyes. "That we need to draw this blackmailer out."

"Have Kristoff come back and do it again and hope someone makes another recording?" She sounded confused.

"No," Alejandro said, catching on to the idea. "Kristoff has been recorded. He has served his purpose. It is interesting that whomever recorded him chose to give the DVD not to him, but to *you.*"

"Exactly," Del chimed in. "The blackmailer is trying to get to you. He or she wants *you* to suffer. Kristoff is just one avenue."

"So what are you suggesting I do?"

One more time, Alejandro and Del exchanged a meaningful glance.

"I think, *querida*, he's suggesting that I arrange a scene for you here and see if we can track him through another disc and 'watch me' note. Or better yet, catch him red-handed in the act of filming you."

Shanna's jaw dropped. "Are you insane! You think I should come here and get naked and..."

"Spend a little time showing our members what you enjoy," Alejandro supplied.

"I can't give this creep any more ammunition to ruin me."

"He already has everything he needs to discredit you with the judges. But I do not think he's actually trying to prevent you from competing, as much as he's attacking you. This feels personal, not professional. If you want to find out who is behind this, you must...expose yourself."

"I'm not into that!"

After last night, Alejandro knew better, but now wasn't the time to remind her. "Perhaps not. Pretend, if you must. But I believe the plan will work."

Shanna hesitated, as if she was pondering his words. "*If* I agree to this crazy scheme, can I do...whatever it is alone?"

Alejandro couldn't resist the grin spreading across his face. "Yes. Plenty of our members would jump through rings of fire to see you touch yourself."

"You mean, like, masturbate for an audience?" She turned ghostly white.

"Even the thought of it makes me hard," he whispered for her ears alone.

"Absolutely not!"

"I will be more than happy to assist you," Alejandro volunteered.

"Yeah, I'll bet."

"It would be more believable and more blackmail-worthy if Ali helped you," Del chimed in. "I will hide in the room and watch all doors, windows, and passersby—see if I can identify our camera-wielding asshole."

Her jaw dropped. "It's bad enough to contemplate getting naked with the Latin Lover, here. But having you watch? Oh, no."

That horror on her face was nothing but a lie. Her suddenly hard nipples told him that. She was scared—of herself, of him, of whatever was fueling her ambition. Suddenly, he wanted to get to the bottom of it all.

"What troubles you? Is the idea too arousing?"

Shanna sent Alejandro a hard glare. "No, it's too weird. And it won't work."

"What are your better ideas?"

Pausing, Shanna bit her lip. Oh, yes, she was thinking her options through.

A few moments later, she gritted her teeth. "I don't have a better idea. But there's got to be one."

"This guy will return to the scene of the crime if we dangle the right bait in front of him. Catching him in the act of creating or delivering a disc is the only way to be certain he's the guilty party."

Pacing across the floor, her tight ass outlined in white Capri pants that made his tongue melt, Shanna contemplated in a silence broken only by her high-heeled sandals.

"God, I can't believe I'm actually considering this. I must be out of my mind."

"It may be the only way to figure out who's trying to screw up your career," Del supplied.

"Which is the only reason I'm considering it."

"Would you feel more comfortable if I showed you the room and all the places Del can hide in order to catch this bastard?"

Del sent him a knowing smile.

She nodded. "I'm not sure this will work, but maybe, seeing the room, something will occur to me."

"You two come up with the plan and let me know. I need to get back to my...company." Del clapped him on the back, kissed Shanna's hand again and disappeared upstairs.

In charged silence, Alejandro led Shanna down a hall and up another set of stairs that led to the play rooms. At the second door on the left, he paused and eased it open into a dark room.

Beyond the handful of comfortable chairs and a long, cushy sofa, lay the far corner of the room, which comprised the stage, currently devoid of guests. The muted lights in that corner shined down on a sleek bed with four chrome posts and matching restraints.

"Oh." Her voice fluttered beside him.

Alejandro would bet this week's take that Shanna was envisioning herself on that stage, her pussy shoved full of his cock—and a rapt audience watching. He'd bet next week's take that she was more aroused than she'd ever been.

"Other members sit here or look through the windows at the far end of the room and watch the scene. From the clip you showed me, I suspect your blackmailer sat in the room, here." Alejandro pointed to a small chair in the shadows, a mere three feet from the end of the bed. "He either used a zoom lens or moved the chair closer to the bed to get the tight penetration shots. But we won't know for sure until we catch him."

"I understand." Her voice trembled even more.

Alejandro smiled to himself as he turned and pointed to a bare wall. "Through here is a doorway, accessible only from the security area. See, no knob on this side. We can position the cameras to watch this chair. Del can either watch the room from the bank of cameras or from the chairs in the far corner."

"I see." She cleared her throat. "If you have security cameras viewing this room, can't you review the footage and see if anyone holding a video camera is in the shot?"

He shook his head. "They point only at the stage areas. Our primary concern here is for the safety of the players. We make sure everything that happens on stage is consensual. If there's a hint that something is not, we bust in. But we do not regularly monitor the audience. For our scene only, we will change the camera positioning."

"Wouldn't the blackmailer be able to spot Del if he was watching from one of those chairs?" She gestured across the room.

"Come with me." Alejandro held out his hand to her.

Shanna looked at it then looked at him, before reluctantly

placing her hand in his. Immediately, sparks danced in his palm, down his fingers. God, he could hardly wait to get his hands on this woman.

For the moment, he led her across the room instead, to a dark pair of padded armchairs. He gestured for Shanna to sit in one. He plunked down in the other.

"In this corner, the light is too dim for anyone in the audience to discern more than a shadow. Players cannot see back in this corner. It's a good place for Del to hide, if you want him nearby."

"It's dark."

A click and a whoosh alerted Alejandro to the fact the players' stage door had opened. He glanced at his watch. Noon. Right on time.

In walked a broad man dressed in leather pants, a half-mask—and nothing else. Colorful tattoos covered his left arm. He held hands with a woman, clutching her fingers in his.

As small as he was big, as delicate as he was strong, the petite redhead followed him to the bed. She wore a flowing floral skirt that ended at mid-thigh, a button-down blouse in a soft ivory and a pair of pink high-heeled sandals.

"Are you wearing a bra, slut?" he asked.

"No, Master."

"Show me."

Without pause, she unbuttoned her blouse to reveal a flat stomach, fair skin and pink nipples that stood straight out and begged for attention.

Shanna gasped. "We shouldn't be watching this."

"They come here knowing that being watched is not only possible, but probable. It turns them on. Shh."

"Good," Master praised, petting one of her breasts in

reward. "Are you wearing panties?"

"No, Master."

"Show me."

The small woman lifted her skirt to reveal slender thighs and a pussy devoid of all hair. Beside Alejandro, Shanna tensed.

"Excellent." The Master cupped her mound and fondled her. "Who do you belong to?"

"You, Master."

"Who decides what's right for your body?"

"You, Master."

"Take off your skirt, lie back, and spread your legs."

The woman complied without hesitation. Even at this distance, once her thighs parted, Alejandro could see a little silver bar passing through the hood of her clit.

"Oh my God," Shanna whispered. "She's...pierced."

"Yes," Alejandro answered. "He marked her. Shh."

"Pretty," said the man in leather as he stared. "Has it healed?"

"Yes, Master."

"Does it arouse you when you walk?"

"Yes, Master."

"Do you rub yourself and make yourself come?"

"No, Master. You did not give me permission."

"That's right. I did not. You're wet."

"Yes, Master."

"Do you need to be fucked?"

"Yes, Master. Please," the redhead pleaded.

The large man said nothing. He merely walked to all four

corners of the bed, restraining his submissive into the built-in cuffs.

"As a reward for your obedience, you will be well fucked." Master snapped his fingers.

In walked another man, completely naked. Young, blond, somewhat thin—but very well hung.

"This is Micah. He will fuck you now. If you please him and obey me, you may suck my cock as a reward. Do you understand?"

"Yes, Master." The idea clearly excited her, and she smiled.

Shanna gripped the arms of her chair and stared at the trio with wide eyes. "She's going to let a complete stranger have sex with her just because he said so?"

"He wants to watch her be fucked, and she has given him domain over her body. She obeys his commands. That is their relationship. Shh."

By now, the blond man had a condom on his long cock and was easing onto the bed.

"Micah," the man barked. "Test that piercing first. With your tongue."

Micah smiled. "With pleasure."

"I will tell you when you have permission to come, slut."

"Yes, Master," she panted as Micah took his first swipe across her clit with his tongue and groaned.

The woman lifted her hips to Micah, who used the opportunity to fit his arms under her thighs and grip her, holding her wet folds against his mouth. He licked her unmercifully, insistent lashes with his tongue, and toyed with the little bar piercing the hood of her clit.

Master shucked off his pants, pulled out a wide cock with a pierced head, and stroked slowly as he watched.

Soon, the redhead was flushed and panting, mewling and pleading for release.

"Stop," said Master.

Micah lifted his head slowly, his lips wet and glossy.

The woman whimpered.

"Are you ready for Micah to fuck you?"

"Yes, Master. Please, yes!"

"Good girl. When I give you permission, you may show me how pretty you are when you come as Micah fucks you."

The woman opened her mouth to answer, but Micah thrust ruthlessly inside her sex first, cutting off all speech. Instead, she gasped, then groaned. Before she recovered, Micah plowed into her again. And again. Once more...

"Come," her master commanded.

She gasped as she orgasmed in a spectacular tensing of limbs and jolting of muscles. Micah gritted his teeth, looking like a man hanging by a thread.

"Beautiful. Micah will continue to fuck you while you suck my cock. You do not come again until I do."

"Yes...Master," she said in a breathy, high gasp just before she turned her head and took Master deep in her mouth.

Beside him, Alejandro noticed Shanna squirming in her seat. Around him, the scent of her arousal wafted. She might pretend to be horrified, but her body told him exactly how much she loved what was happening before her eyes. How much she liked watching it. He knew from dancing with her that she ached to be watched herself. No doubt in his mind, fucking her in front of a faceless audience would completely arouse Shanna. She couldn't possibly hang onto her ice bitch persona then.

It didn't take long before Master's buttocks were clenching. He shoved his hand into his slut's red hair and thrust into her mouth. Micah had apparently gotten his urge to come under control and now pounded her like a man possessed, beads of sweat dripping down his face, his sides. The woman's skin was a gorgeous shade of aroused rose as she writhed between the two men, giving and receiving pleasure.

Soon, the Master tensed, shouted, and erupted into her mouth.

"Come," he told them through clenched teeth.

They did. Loudly, bucking and rocking and clearly enjoying the hell out of themselves.

Moments later, Micah withdrew from the woman's body and disposed of his condom. Master reached out and gave him a brotherly handshake.

"She's one hell of a fuck," Micah commented. "You're lucky, man."

Master nodded and smiled. Micah disappeared through the door from which he'd emerged. When Master turned his profile to the audience again, Alejandro had no trouble spotting the fact he was hard again. Shanna's gasp told him she'd seen it, too.

Without a word to his slut, Master released her ankles, flipped her onto her belly. As her arms crossed above her head, he urged her to curl her knees under her body, then smacked her ass a half-dozen times in harsh, rhythmic swats. The woman tensed, moaned, bucked.

Then Master reached for the table on the far side of the bed. Moments later, he had lube on his dick and was sliding it inside his woman's rosy ass.

She moaned and writhed when he penetrated her deep, and he reached around to toy with her clit.

"You're a good girl. Watching you get fucked turns me on,

but fucking you myself is heaven. You accept my cock wherever I put it, don't you?"

"Yes! Master, yes!"

Shanna crossed her legs and squirmed again. "Is he...having anal sex with her?"

Alejandro nodded. "It is another show of her submission to him."

She drew in a sharp breath. Even in this dim light, he could see her hard nipples go even harder. Oh, another something on his long list of things to do to her body once he got the chance. Alejandro managed to keep his smile to himself—barely.

"Seen enough?"

"What?" Shanna tore her eyes away from the couple reluctantly. "O—oh, yes."

He rose and helped her to her feet, then guided her out the door, back into the well-lit hallway. Flushed cheeks, very hard nipples, rapid breaths, pulse beating at her neck. If she owned a vibrator, he'd bet it would get a strenuous workout this afternoon. First time he could ever remember being jealous of plastic and batteries. He'd offer his own flesh, but if he pushed her too hard, too fast, she would run in the other direction.

"So, the scene... How does tomorrow night sound for catching a blackmailer? I will make sure the room is free then."

Shanna took a deep breath. "I haven't made up my mind."

"Whatever you wish. You are the one with a competition in a few weeks and a blackmailer with an ax to grind."

"Damn it. All right. Tomorrow night."

"Be here by nine." Alejandro tamped down his smile of triumph with effort. "What sort of scene should I set up? Something for you to do alone?"

Shanna paled a bit more, then mustered her bravado and lifted her chin. "Maybe...you should participate, too. But don't get the wrong idea."

"Wrong idea?"

She sent him a suspicious glare. "I'm serious. This is business. I need to find out who's trying to sabotage me. You need to know who's jeopardizing your club. I'm not interested in you personally."

"Of course not."

"And I'm not sleeping with you."

Who said anything about sleeping? Alejandro thought fiercely.

"Whatever you want, that is what we'll do. Nothing more." *And absolutely nothing less.*

Chapter Four

"You sure about this, man?" Del asked him at eight-thirty the following night as they headed downstairs.

"Yes." Alejandro led the way down the hall, to the second door on the left, and pushed it open.

Del closed it behind him. "You want guests in here? They will flip. You're the brains of this place. You almost never play in public. You know the curiosity. There *will* be a crowd."

Alejandro shrugged. Generally, he watched rather than was watched, but this was about Shanna tonight, about making her hot. And she adored being watched. He knew that all the way down to the soles of his feet.

"Whatever. Mostly I want anyone here who attended in the last week, especially if they watched in this room. I emailed you a list of known members who fit that description. Start there. I've asked security to do the same. That way, it's more likely our friend with the video camera will show up. But wait until nine-fifteen to unlock the door. I want Shanna comfortable. It will be easier for her to let go the first time if the only one watching when we get started is you."

"Even if we only allow the people who have been in this room in the last week, others will follow. There will still be a crowd."

Alejandro shrugged. Likely so, but he would deal with it. And with Shanna...

She would be very nervous when she first arrived, but Alejandro didn't think that would last. Especially if there wasn't a crowd right away. And God, he couldn't wait to feel her melt against him, her body opening to accept him deep, her pussy clasping him hard as she came. By then, she'd be desperate for the crowd to watch her come undone.

"I need to finish readying the room." Alejandro turned away, eager for the night to begin.

"Wait." When Alejandro turned back, Del went on, "You're going pretty far to catch this blackmailer."

"The club is important. We both have over a million dollars tied up in it. We cannot afford to allow anyone who would videotape players without their knowledge to continue their membership."

"Yeah. Absolutely. It's just...normally you would let security handle it. Or bring in help, if you needed it. This time, you seem to be taking a very personal interest."

"Stop side-stepping around your words. What are you saying?"

Del crossed his arms over his wide chest, looking way too pleased. "You like this girl."

"She is very sexy. Why should I not like her?"

Disbelief peppered Del's expression. "There are sexy women here every night more than willing to fuck you. You haven't played with or performed for the membership in over a year. So there's more to your decision to get on that stage with Shanna than the fact she's sexy."

Mierda. Why couldn't Del leave it alone?

Alejandro sighed. "Yes. I confess, even I am not entirely

sure why I am pursuing Shanna so hard. She has rebuffed, left, and insulted me."

"But...?"

Shifting his weight from one foot to the other, Alejandro sorted through the tangle of his thoughts and feelings. It was damn uncomfortable. He was a gut-instinct sort of guy. If it felt right, he did it. That philosophy had never served him wrong. But even he had to admit that his logic where Shanna was concerned...

There wasn't any.

"She has this lost quality. I don't want to save her, exactly. Or change her. But I cannot resist wanting to hold her. Touch her. And, of course, pleasure her. She looks at me, and her expression is like a siren's song. A glance, and I'm hard as hell. A snap from that icy voice I know is hiding a wealth of heat, and I'm dying to lay her out, get deep, and melt her into a puddle."

Del laughed. "You're screwed."

"I suspect so."

"You're falling for this girl. Hard."

Was it that obvious?

"And you haven't really touched her yet." Del roared with laughter. "This is going to be fun to watch for more than one reason."

"You may fuck off now."

"Ten-four." Del clapped him on the back. "I'll finish making the arrangements with the other employees. The room should be ready. All you need to do is meet Shanna at the door."

No, what he needed to do was please her, not just by lighting her senses and firing her fantasies, but endearing himself to her. Great, but how to do that? Because his gut was telling him now that he should not let Shanna out of his life.

God, she was shaking. Shanna shoved the door open and entered the cool air-conditioned space of Sneak Peek. At night, the club still had that golden glow. But instead of the homey warmth it conveyed during the day, as moonlight spilled into the windows, the club sparkled, glittered, like old Hollywood meeting today's beautiful people, all surrounded by dazzling sex.

Del and Alejandro had captured the club's ambiance perfectly.

Just past the club's front door, wall-to-wall bodies gyrated to a suggestive techno beat. Couples grinded, intimating sex vertically. In fact, one couple against the wall, shielded by the man's long leather duster, probably *was* having sex. No one seemed to notice or care.

The bar beyond was crowded with people drinking their liquid fortification. Several men crowded around a twenty-something woman downing shots, like they were waiting for her to give one—or several—of them a sign that she was ready for action.

The whole place oozed sex.

She *so* didn't belong here. Sex had never been her...thing. She'd had it, of course. A college boyfriend had been her first, but he hadn't had much experience. Nor had he understood her dancing. They'd spent the relationship fighting because he assumed she was sleeping with her dance partner at the time, which she hadn't been.

A few years later, she'd had a one-night stand after a wedding. Stupid—and awful. Downright bad sex.

Jonathan...utter disaster—right on the dance floor they'd practiced on for years. She'd clung to him out of desperation.

He'd taken her body as if exorcising some demon. The whole episode had lasted less than ten minutes. And created months of pure havoc.

By tonight's end, if she wasn't careful, she would be adding Alejandro to the list. She'd said she wouldn't have sex with him. But she wondered... Would failing to have actual sex in public convince this blackmailer that they were for real? Not likely. It would probably look like a trap. They had to ferret out this jerk before the California Dance Star.

Shanna sighed. But that wasn't the only reason for contemplating surrendering to Alejandro. Could she actually resist a man that sinfully sexy, especially when he was seducing her by fulfilling her secret exhibitionism fantasy? He made her feel sexual, made her believe that he understood her. Admitting that fact was painful, but even when Alejandro annoyed her, he turned her on. Maybe...the chemistry between them was worth exploring.

And maybe she was out of her mind.

Crossing the room, Shanna was conscious of male eyes following her. God, why had Alejandro sent her this sheer halter top, held in place by nothing more than two little bows, along with a matching wrap-around skirt? Insisted she wear a skimpy outfit in shades of soft creamy-gold that blended in with her skin?

"Hi," a voice whispered in her ear. She turned to find a guy with dimples and incredible blue eyes visually eating her up. "Dance?"

Okay, he was attractive. Who was she kidding? He was gorgeous. The way he looked at her made her burn. But to dance with him? Touch him? Hmm. The thought of getting physical with this guy—with most any guy—wasn't quite as tempting. For her, it was always that way.

Except with Alejandro.

"I—I…"

"She's spoken for tonight."

Alejandro. She recognized that deep, slightly accented voice caressing the back of her neck. And the tingle that shimmied up her spine when he wrapped his arm around her bare midriff in a gesture designed to lay his claim.

Dimples shot her a brief look of regret. "Sure, Mr. Diaz."

"She'll be around later, in the chrome room."

That information perked Dimples up. He raked her with a lingering glance. "Sweet. I'll definitely be watching."

Before Shanna could protest, Alejandro urged her forward to an employees-only entrance and shut the door behind them. The decibel level went down about a thousand percent.

She whirled to face him "You *invited* him to watch us…?"

Shanna was glad she'd managed to parlay her anger into actual words quickly. Because once she saw his casual black shirt unbuttoned all the way down the front, exposing a healthy glimpse of hard-steel pecs and smooth bronze skin, she lost her train of thought.

"To play. Yes, I did. He is one of the newer regulars and he was here last week. Think of him as a potential suspect."

His voice brought her gaze back up to his face, where a hint of a smile played. The bastard knew she'd been staring at him.

She needed dispassion, not lust. *Focus.* "He had no idea who I was. No concept that I'm Kristoff's partner."

"Not that he let on. But if he was guilty, why would he tip his hand?"

Good question. One for which she had no answer.

"Do you want to change your mind? You are not required to play this scene."

Of course she was. If she wanted to win the competition and hold that trophy in her hand after sixteen years of hard work, she did. But that wasn't the only reason. If she wanted to find out if she was capable of feeling great pleasure in a man's arms, she had to go through with this. If she wanted to find out if Alejandro had been right about her desire to exhibit and see how deeply he understood her...well, then she couldn't chicken out now.

"Just lead the way."

With a slow nod, Alejandro grabbed her hand and gave it a reassuring squeeze, then led her down the hall. Despite her nerves, Shanna had a hard time ripping her gaze from his tight ass, displayed so mouth-wateringly in black slacks. The view alone made her want to jump him. That had to stop. This strong sexual hunger wasn't like her. Being too into him wasn't a good idea.

Tearing her gaze away and focusing on her surroundings, she noticed they filed past some open doors containing offices brimming with computers manned by staff members. A wall clock said it was ten 'til nine.

The butterflies in her stomach were head banging and had set up a mosh pit. She wondered if she was going to throw up before they got started.

Alejandro stopped in front of a door. "Relax. You will be fine. We're going to handle this together."

"Why are you being nice about this?"

He cocked a brow, the strong angles of his face dusted by shadow. The frankly sexual stare he sent her made Shanna suck in her breath.

"Certainly, it has not escaped your notice that I want you."

How could it when the thought thrilled her so much? She shook her head.

"Good. I also want to catch the scum taking advantage of our members. You want to catch him, too, so Kristoff's DVD doesn't fall into the judges' hands. It is a win-win for us both."

That made sense.

He hesitated. "And I suspect you're not the untouchable bitch you wish me—and everyone else—to believe you are." He shot her a wolfish grin. "But I will find out tonight if that's true. We are going to be very hot together."

Before she could protest and put up the armor he'd stripped away with a single sentence, he thrust the door open and walked through.

They entered the room she had observed the Master and slut use yesterday. Only, things had changed. The chrome bed had been pushed to one corner, at the edge of the stage. The rest of the furniture had been moved out, leaving a large amount of the painted concrete floor well-lit and totally empty. The bedding had changed as well. Luxurious white and silvery linens with fluffy pillows decorated with beads and tassels adorned the bed, looking sumptuous on top of the downy blanket. A far cry from yesterday's stark black sheets.

"What's this?"

"I thought you would be more comfortable if we changed the room up to something softer. Something more...you."

Normally, she would protest his judgment that she was soft. But he was right; the look of the room did reflect her more. Again, she wondered how he already knew her so unerringly.

She was touched, against her better judgment. "Thank you."

"You are very welcome. Come with me." Alejandro tugged

her to the edge of the stage. Deep in gray shadows, she saw a lone, imposing figure.

"Hi, Shanna."

"Del?"

"Yes. We're ready to go. Are you okay?"

She managed to resist the urge to press a hand against her fluttering belly. It would reveal too much, make her look vulnerable. She already felt too much that way for comfort. "Yes."

"Good. The security cameras have been positioned to watch the audience, specifically the corner in which we think the last video was made. The lighting in the audience is a bit brighter, so the cameras can capture whatever is going on. None of the cameras will be pointed at you, and Alejandro will take care of you if something unexpected happens. Security is through that door." He pointed to the door without a handle. "Just knock, and they'll let you in immediately."

Wow, they'd thought of everything. "Thank you."

"We will start slow," Alejandro assured her. "Right now, just you and me. Del will watch. As you get comfortable, he'll open the door. Hopefully, your blackmailer will be waiting to get in."

Del watching them. Other strangers watching them. Now came the hard part. And the arousing part. She wished the thought of Alejandro touching her didn't turn her on...almost as much as she wished the thought of a crowd seeing their every move didn't make her blood race.

But it all did. Unbearably. And Alejandro knew it.

Shanna bit her lip. "O—okay."

"Good." Alejandro smiled, something ripe with both warmth and fire. In one look, he managed to calm her fears and rouse her body.

Shanna had a feeling this night would be unlike anything she could have possibly imagined.

She glanced at Del. He was a big shape sitting in the dark corner, his head cocked, his arms crossed over his chest.

"Focus on me, *querida*. Me."

Right. She gave him a shaky nod, and he tugged on her hand, pulling her body into his.

"Dance with me."

"D—dance?"

"Just dance."

He snapped his fingers. Music filtered through the room, a soft but spicy Latin tune, perfect for a rumba. In fact, it was the music they had danced to just a few nights before.

As Alejandro led her into a basic, her body brushing his with every step, her feet moved automatically to the beat. His unbuttoned shirt fluttered as he moved, offering tantalizing glimpses of hard pectorals, flat, brown nipples, hints of dark hair. Her mind whirled with tempting possibilities.

"You recall the exact music we danced to the other night?"

"I never forget a thing about you."

Seven words and she melted. On the spot. No man had ever taken such an interest in just her. Only in whether she could win. Only in her abilities, her ambition...never in her as a woman.

Shanna relaxed against him and drifted into the dance. He sensed it and spiced up their steps. After a sharp turn in his arms, her nearly bare back rested against his half-covered chest, his hot breath on her neck, her hips gyrating against his erection. His palm flattened against her naked belly, which pulsed at his hot touch.

She turned her head, glancing over her shoulder at him.

His fiery gaze was full of challenge as he slowly caressed her until both of his hands came to rest at her hips, guiding them in a movement that was pure, raw sex.

"Del is watching us. Watching you. Getting hard for you," he whispered.

"No," she protested automatically.

But her blood boiled at the thought.

Alejandro turned her out in a sharp spin and brought her crashing into his body again, then into a deep dip.

Her gaze snapped up to his. His face shouted dominance, mastery. "Yes."

Her nipples went hard.

As he brought her up slowly, he curled one hand around her nape. The other he flattened between her breasts, then pressed over one. He teased her nipple with a soft touch.

Shanna sucked in a breath. Desire dropped like a bomb into the pit of her stomach. That strong face of his...all hint of teasing, of reassuring, of politeness—gone. In his place stood a man who meant to have her. Sooner than now.

He fitted his hips against hers and rocked as his lips collided with hers. A brush, a slide, a taste. Shanna followed his lead, shocked at the way her heart accelerated like a race car, zooming to hyper-speed in seconds until it pounded in her ears. He tasted of coffee and man and aggression. She opened to him, desperate for him to sink deeper.

Instead, he spun her out. She whirled away from him on instinct.

The rumba was the dance of love...but there was teasing involved. The woman hesitating, the man pursuing. Somehow she knew Alejandro loved to pursue.

The last thing she should do was make her surrender too

easy for him.

She walked away, hips swaying, head held high. For a moment, she focused on Del. He leaned forward in his chair, his posture tense. His fingers clutched the chair in front of him. She smiled, writhed, and caressed her way between her breasts, down her belly, skirting her aching sex to caress the tops of her thighs. She heard Del's indrawn breath when the music paused.

Feminine power, heady and amazing, crashed into her. This was why she loved dancing, knowing she could make men want, people feel, just by watching her body.

Then she glanced over her shoulder as Alejandro prowled closer, shedding his black shirt, leaving it forgotten on the floor. Powerful bronze shoulders snagged her gaze. His hard-muscled chest narrowed into six-pack abs dusted with a treasure trail that disappeared into the waistband of his pants. The enticing view made her mouth water. But the look on his face...hungry, unrepentant, demanding, made her shudder with want.

Damn, she was staring—and loving it.

Alejandro stopped directly behind her, so close, she could feel the heat of his body. Even though he didn't touch her, he sucked her deeper into his sexual web just by being near and sharing the rhythm of the dance.

Suddenly...a tug, a brush of his fingers. The little halter top fell to the floor at her feet.

Leaving her naked from the waist up.

Instinctively, she reached up to cover her breasts with her hands. Alejandro slid his palms down her arms, skin to skin, until his hands covered hers. He rocked against her ass, his erection insistent at her lower back. He planted teasing kisses down her neck, across her shoulder.

Tension tightened in her belly. Resistance melted.

Then he forced her hands down, over her ribs, down her belly, right over her swollen, aching folds. His hips swiveled to the music, moving hers in time—grinding her clit into her fingertips.

"Jesus," Del muttered from the audience.

Shanna barely heard. Sensation exploded. She gasped as the riot of feelings tore through her, leaving fire in its wake. Her knees melted. Her head fell back to Alejandro's bare shoulder. Her eyes closed as she moaned.

One of his hands swept across her abdomen again, soft, slow...inching up, up... Until Alejandro claimed her bare breast, his palm burning her sensitive flesh. Shanna's eyes fluttered open. The way he touched her with that slow burn compelled her to look.

Del watched their every move, his gaze riveted on Alejandro's hand moving over her skin. Shanna knew Del saw her arousal, knew he wasn't missing the fact she was spiked up on need and desire. Aching. And it was only climbing higher, knowing that Del couldn't peel his eyes away.

Her nipple poked Alejandro's palm. She ached, arched into his hand as his thumb teased the hard tip.

"Touch me," she whispered.

"Every last inch of you." Alejandro's mouth strung a fresh line of shiver-inducing kisses up her neck.

Suddenly, he grabbed one of her hands, twirled her out, then reeled her back in, her chest crushed to his. Slowly, he eased her away in a rumba rhythm.

His hazel eyes flared as he took in his first clear glimpse of her bare breasts.

"Such hard pink nipples. I'm going to enjoy making them red."

Wondering how he could all but made her heart stop. "H— how? By pinching them?"

He reached between their bodies and slid heated palms over her breasts. His thumbs cradled their aching tips as his fingers closed in and pressed, jolting her with a flash of pain, followed by a haze of pleasure.

"That is one way."

"And b—by sucking them?"

His gaze was like an inferno burning her up as he dipped her back over his arm, arching her breasts toward his mouth, fusing their hips together. God, she could feel every inch of his thick erection pressing right against her sex. She ached in a way she never had before and never imagined she could.

Then he lowered his head and sucked her nipple into his mouth.

Hot. Wet. Wild. Thrilling. Sensations screamed through her body as he suckled her, his mouth pulling, tugging, creating friction that zipped right from her breast to her clit until pleasure tightened, converged, pounded at her body.

Shanna clutched his shoulders, praying the sensation would never end.

After a long, lingering lick, Alejandro eased away from her breast and stood her upright again. "That is another possibility."

"Do you... W—would you bite them?"

He didn't even answer, just bent to capture her breast in his mouth again, the hot silk of his tongue over the sensitive bud giving way to the tug of teeth—and a bolt of pure fire straight down to her sex.

Oh God.

"Yes!" The word slipped out of her mouth. Surrender in one

syllable. She knew it. So did he.

She was going to give him anything—everything—he wanted tonight.

Alejandro straightened and smiled down at her. That expression captured her, but he enthralled her when he slid his fingers into her hair, scattering the pins holding her French twist everywhere, and ravaged her mouth.

Need, impatience, aggression, the promise of unbelievable sex—it was all there in his kiss. His tongue stroked hers and stoked the fires leaping inside her, sending her higher and higher.

Alejandro had barely touched anything below her waist, and already she was screamingly close to orgasm. He'd already brought her closer to the pinnacle than any of her other previous lovers. Damn, what would happen when he actually laid her down on that sumptuous bed and covered her body with his? When he filled her up with every inch he taunted her with even now as he rocked against her?

Panting, mewling, Shanna grabbed his face with clutching fingers and pressed her lips harder against his. God, it was stupid and dangerous...and she couldn't wait to find out just how good he was going to be.

Chapter Five

Shanna panted, clinging to Alejandro when he lodged his thigh between hers and urged her to swivel her hips against him.

Thick bolts of need speared her belly, slicing down her legs. Her blood turned thick. The wanton within her demanded more. Shanna aimed to make sure she got it.

She wasn't the Bitch of the Ballroom tonight. She was just a female surrendering to the hot sensations her lover's touch roused. How it happened, she didn't know. Why now and with this man, in this situation, was a mystery, too. But for once, she felt like a woman. Not just an athlete, a dancer, or a competitor. Just a woman in touch with her sexuality.

Orgasm approached hard and fast. Tension built between her legs. Heat fractured her thoughts. She moaned, feeling Alejandro's hands at her hips, urging her on, and Del's hot stare burning her back.

As she climbed up, up, Alejandro lifted his mouth from hers and sent her a deliciously wicked smile. God, the man could melt steel with that look. And she was nowhere near that solid.

"You ache." He didn't ask; he stated.

"Yes."

"You are wet."

No doubt, he felt her wet folds through the thin fabric of his slacks, and the friction it provided was driving her out of her mind.

"Yes."

Then he reached around her, gliding rough palms over her bare ass as he lifted her skirt to her waist. Shanna knew Del could see her cheeks and the delicate white thong bisecting them. She swore she could feel his stare burning her backside. And she knew it affected him because he groaned.

That sound reached between her legs and jolted her. Why it turned her on so much to excite Del she couldn't explain. And didn't want to know. Tomorrow, she'd likely be mortified. Tonight, she just didn't care.

"Do you like knowing that Del is eating up your ass with his hungry gaze?" Alejandro rasped in her ear. "That he's so hard for you and would kill to be in my place right now?"

Shanna couldn't help it; she whimpered.

"That's right. But he will not touch you. He will watch and he will want, but *I* will take every sinful pleasure your body has to offer."

The man flat knew how to talk. With a few choice words, he utterly unwound her.

Then he tugged on the skirt's tie, slipped free the button. Her skirt fluttered to the stage. She wore only one very damp thong.

He lowered his hands to her hips again, forcing her sex down on his thigh once more. To the music, they swayed. His impressive erection brushed her belly. Her need to come grew, expanded until she was moaning, muttering words of nonsense and need.

"Please. Please!"

"I will give you everything you can take. Then I will give you more."

He barely finished whispering the promise when he bent her back over his arm, arching her breasts up so he could feast on them again. Her nipples were so hard under his tongue, and no matter how he licked, suckled, bit, she only wanted more.

Shanna had never been greedy with sex. Never really wanted sex. To be so lost in the moment, in the sensation— stunning, amazing. For all the time she'd wondered if she was "normal" because she didn't respond to a man's touch, she now had her answer. She responded to Alejandro. To Del's eyes on her. To the forbidden burn of everything they had planned tonight.

Still bent over Alejandro's arm, Shanna opened her eyes to lock her stare with Del's, to entice him with what he couldn't have. And though the room was upside down from this vantage, she could not miss the small crowd filing in. Men. More than five, less than a dozen, they all had tense bodies, hot eyes.

"Fuck, she's hot," murmured a total stranger.

Del stood in the middle of them, fists clenched at his sides. "She is that."

"They want you," Alejandro murmured against her neck. "And I want to show them what they're missing."

Before she could even process what he meant, Alejandro spun her around to face the audience. Oh, God, they stood a mere three feet away. So close she swore she could feel their hot breaths on her skin. She recognized Dimples there. His smile was gone, replaced by seething want and an erection a blind woman could not miss.

He and the rest of the crowd were focused on her bare breasts, loose and heavy as Alejandro forced her hips to maintain the rhythm of the music.

Collective groans rushed up, mirroring the rush of desire inside her. Could she actually come simply from being watched?

Since she frequently had trouble orgasming during masturbation, the thought of simply letting loose here, now, was a wild, heady one.

Alejandro slid his palms down her arms, still behind her, rocking to the beat of the music. Then he lifted her hands above her head until they encircled his neck.

Another chorus of groans erupted from the audience. A quick glance down proved the new pose raised her breasts, made her nipples stand straight out like an invitation.

"Don't move," Alejandro commanded. "Just feel. Just let go."

She gave him a shaky nod, wondering, eager—aching—for whatever he planned next.

Shanna didn't have to wait long. A moment later, his fingertips trailed down the side of her breast, across the flat of her abdomen, and disappeared right into her wet thong.

He gave her no time to absorb the fact he was fondling her in public—and that she loved it—before his fingers zeroed in on her clit. A brush, a rub. An amazing spark. Tingles danced through her sex, in her belly, down her thighs. The tension ratcheted up until she could barely breathe.

"You going to come for them?" Alejandro whispered in her ear.

She nodded erratically.

"You going to come for me?"

"Yes!" She bit her lip to keep from screaming as the ache deepened into something nearly unbearable.

With the music throbbing in her ears, Alejandro's fingers shoving her past the breaking point, with nearly a dozen sets of hot male eyes and thoughts enveloped in only her, Shanna came apart.

Her hoarse cry erupted above the music. Her eyes closed, and pleasure washed over her, sharp, golden, unbelievable.

Nothing had ever been like that. Nothing had ever prepared her for the addicting rush of pure sensation lighting up her body. *Oh. My. God.*

Alejandro took her down slowly before extracting his hand from her panties. When he did, she looked down to find his fingers soaked with her cream.

He gave a satisfied chuckle in her ear. "This is how I want you. Dripping wet for me."

She gasped as he anointed her nipples with her juice, then whirled her to face him. With long, languid swipes of his tongue, he licked her taste away with a moan that reverberated deep inside her, stirring the ache back to life.

Shanna was shocked when he stepped away and took her hand in his. Suddenly, she was aware of being almost totally bare, while everyone around her was half-clothed or more. She *felt* naked. Vulnerable. Yet oddly strong. She glanced between Alejandro and the tense, shuffling audience.

"That's it?"

He leaned in, looking to the world like a lover planting soft kisses just below her ear. "If you want it to be. We certainly gave the blackmailer something to film."

Yes, but was it enough? And was that really the reason she was contemplating the words about to come out of her mouth?

"I want more."

Alejandro pulled back enough to glance down into her face,

his stare delving deep down into hers. "Are you sure?"

All she knew was that she wasn't ready for tonight to end. She nodded.

Gently, he grabbed her wrist and placed her hand over his erection. Damn, he was hard. And very large. Oh, wow...

"I'm dying to feel you around me," he whispered. "Your mouth, your pussy... Tell me what you want. How much of you will you give me?"

The real question was, could she actually hold anything back?

Shanna felt her way up his cock, to the catch of his slacks. She flipped it open, and he sucked in a harsh breath. Another groan from the audience spurred her on. With slow torture in mind, she eased down his zipper, taking her sweet time.

"If you have a 'no' on the tip of your tongue, say it now."

Shanna leaned closer to his primal male heat, her mouth hovering above the hard nub of his brown nipple. She flicked a sultry gaze up to his face, latching onto his burning stare. "Never heard the word."

Brazen. When had she ever been that? Or aggressive or hungry or dying to feel a man's animal heat burning her up? Never. For years, she'd poured her passion into dance. When she performed, she could express all her pent-up feelings through the movements of her body and the interaction with her partner. In real life...she'd never put a tenth of her passion into sex. Tonight—now—she wanted to change all that.

Alejandro had compelled her to.

She closed her mouth around his nipple and nibbled him with her teeth. He groaned long and loud. Holding in her satisfied smile, she pushed his pants down over his hips, sliding them down his thighs.

His sex sprang free, so hard it nearly lay against his belly. So long, it reached toward his navel. So thick, she wondered if she could actually get her hand all the way around it. So perfect, she knew that once he sank deep into her, she'd know the most amazing pleasure, not just of her life, but beyond her fantasies.

Shanna fell to her knees. She could hardly wait.

When his slacks reached his ankles, Alejandro was very glad he hadn't bothered with anything underneath.

He was even more glad to see Shanna on her knees, eyeing his cock.

Alejandro took himself in hand and guided the weeping head closer to the red haven of her lush mouth.

He barely anchored his palm around the crown of her head when she opened wide to take inch after inch inside the stunning, wet heat as she cradled him on her tongue. *Dios mío!*

She sucked hard, and he felt her all over his cock. The head nudged the back of her throat. Her tongue swiped the sensitive underside of his cock, swirled around the swollen head.

Heaven; she was exactly that. Sleek. She was built for long, sweaty, intense fucks—and to show off for the audience that would soon masturbate to the sounds of her orgasm.

About that, he had no doubt.

To his left, the audience watched. Moaned. A few guys were adjusting themselves. Others had given up and were already stroking their own cocks. A few women had wandered into the room, and he hoped they understood there would likely be a line a mile long to fuck them if they stayed.

Then Shanna drew back, her tongue laving the head of his

cock, igniting a maelstrom of icy-hot tingles in his balls, down his spine. He stopped thinking completely. Too full of sensation now, he fucked her mouth slowly as she whimpered around him, her fingers locked on his thighs...slowly inching up to his ass.

She took him to the back of her throat again. Her nails dug into his skin, and the hint of pain pushed him closer to the edge of pleasure. Damn, he was going to come if she kept that up.

A part of him wanted to rush into the ache and explode on her tongue, down her throat, just for the joy of watching her take him, swallow him.

But he wanted to fuck her more. Way more.

Gritting his teeth, Alejandro pulled out of her mouth. She protested with an unintelligible groan, but he bent and grabbed her waist, lifting her until she stood. Whirling her away from him, to face the tall, chrome bed post, he forced her to bend toward it. Then with his fingers over hers, he clasped her hands around the pole.

"Hold on. You will need to," he growled in her ear.

Bending quickly, he found the condom in his pocket and rolled it on, counting the torturous heartbeats until he could be balls deep in the sweet heat of her pussy. Seven seconds. That's all it took until he gripped her hips and thrust inside her.

Scalding hot. Fist tight. *Madre de Dios,* he wasn't going to last. But by damn, she was going over the edge first.

Bracketing harsh fingers on her hips, he pushed his way inside. Shoved hard. It seemed to take forever. Her pussy was so swollen, and if he had to guess, she had not had sex in months, maybe longer.

That was going to change. No way would tonight be the last time he fucked her. No way would he wait weeks, or even days, to feel this again. She'd be lucky if he would wait hours.

The way he felt at the moment, he did not think such luck was on her side.

Jacked up on an overload of sensation and a burning need to come brewing at the base of his spine, Alejandro took a deep breath and plunged into her slowly. Hell, it wasn't helping his concentration to see guys jacking off to the sight of Shanna's naked body. Or one of the women in the room with her skirt around her waist and a man's cock buried inside her as she straddled his lap.

Tearing his gaze away, he focused on the long line of Shanna's naked spine, her mussed golden tresses spilling across her narrow back. He couldn't *not* touch her.

Lifting one hand off her hip, he reached around her body and toyed with her breasts, pinching one of her responsive nipples. She gasped, and Alejandro felt his primitive side take over. He sank his teeth into her neck. He squeezed her other nipple. Her body responded instinctively, tightening on his cock. She was close.

Thank God. So was he.

Gliding his palm down her belly, he buried his fingers into the sparse curls between her legs. *There.* Her clit stood up, hard and swollen, pleading for attention. He wasn't about to say no.

He swiped his fingers across her bundle of nerves. She moaned, tightened again. The friction of moving inside her was about to blow the top off his head. But he kept moving.

"Do you see them watching you?" he snarled, on the edge. "Do you see them wanting you?"

"Yes," she cried. "Yes."

"I want you more."

"Oh, God," she gasped. "Alejandro!"

He strummed her clit once more. "You are going to come."

Damn, he was trying so hard to hold it together, he was cross-eyed and slurring his words. But she understood.

"Yes!"

And then she did, clamping down on him, massaging his cock with the pulsing walls of her sex. His self-control didn't stand a chance.

The sensation started deep in his gut and dropped with heavy need right into his balls. Pleasure climbed up, up, up his cock until he found himself shouting his throat raw in release.

He clutched her tight, pumping his way through utopia, with just one thought rattling through his fevered brain:

Mine.

Chapter Six

Tango music throbbed—kind of like Shanna's head. The insistent beat of the dramatic music echoed off the hardwood floors and bounced off the mirrored walls of the studio. Her feet ached. She was hot and sweaty after three hours. And really annoyed. She and Kristoff were *not* having a productive practice.

And as much as she hated to admit it, Alejandro kept invading her thoughts every three seconds. How could she miss him so much after a mere two days? Why couldn't she stop thinking about the way his hands felt on her, his unique scent that smelled like midnight and man, all wrapped in pure sex. Why hadn't she stopped remembering the way he'd looked at her—as if she meant something—before she thrust her clothes on in a rush. Why could she still see hurt on Alejandro's face when, a few minutes later, she abruptly darted out his door?

"I have never had to say this to you," Kristoff broke into her thoughts, "but if we are going to win, you must concentrate. You know this, yes? The tango, it is strong and passionate, not lethargic and distracted."

Damn Kristoff for stepping on her last nerve.

Shanna thrust her hands on her hips. "If I'm distracted, it's because I'm still trying to figure out how we're going to keep that DVD of yours out of the judges' hands. And guess what?

The fact that's even a problem is not my fault."

"I made a mistake. I have apologized. Either forgive me or find a new partner. Or have you been holding auditions behind my back?"

In the past, that comment alone would have been enough to push her over the edge. She would have told Kristoff to spend his time at Sneak Peek and stop wasting hers. Then she would have begun auditioning partners the very same day. She didn't need this crap. Seriously.

So why didn't she walk away?

Kristoff was, in a word, amazing. A powerful dancer, determined, dedicated. He brought a glamour to their dancing she'd been lacking with Jonathan. The ladies loved him. He oozed charm even when making his matador face during the Paso Doble. He was spirited, and normally, he made practice fun. And yes, she wanted to find a partner with whom she could finish her career.

That wasn't why she didn't want to lose Kristoff, though. During their time together, he'd become...almost a friend. She tried very hard not to bring her emotions into her dance partnerships, but Shanna knew he hadn't intended to make a mess of things. She hated the thought of turning her back on him and proving his suspicions about her right.

In the past, it had never bothered her to be known as the Bitch of the Ballroom. Now, for some reason...it bothered her. A lot.

"Shut up and dance," she snapped.

"We can still win."

They could, if they didn't have the DVD hovering over their heads. But why bring it up again? It wouldn't change their situation. Still, she usually would have added the dig just to remind him exactly how he'd screwed up. Today, she didn't have petty in her, not when there was a bit of kicked puppy in his expression.

Damn it, had the handful of orgasms Alejandro had given her softened her that much? Shanna stiffened her spine. She couldn't afford to think with her heart—not if she wanted to win. And winning was all she had, even if it sounded so...empty. No, she was just tired or something. She'd worked too hard to lose focus now.

If she couldn't figure out who was behind this blackmail before the competition, she was going to have to cut Kristoff loose. Period.

"We can win if we get that DVD out of circulation. I'm working on that."

"Is that why you went to Sneak Peek and performed a public scene with Alejandro Diaz?"

Shanna nearly choked. It hadn't occurred to her that Kristoff would find out. In retrospect, she should have known better. He was a member there. Clearly, someone had told him.

He laughed. "I heard it was very hot and that you had a rapt audience."

"I did what needed to be done."

Yeah, she'd done whatever she had to in order to achieve that first orgasm, and the second. She'd barely resisted his offer of a third, which he'd promised to give her in his bed, just the two of them on soft satin sheets.

Bad girl!

"And you did it very well, I hear."

Shanna rolled her eyes and turned away so he wouldn't see her cheeks turning pink.

But she wasn't fast enough.

"You're blushing. You?" Astonishment laced Kristoff's voice.

"I have never seen you do such a thing."

It was rare, and all because Alejandro had blown her away, and she wasn't sure she had recovered yet. She had never craved sex or ached for any man. Until Alejandro. Last night, before she'd lost herself to the sensations of self-pleasure, she'd wondered exactly what Alejandro had done to her and why she was so fascinated by him.

How was it possible he'd gotten under her skin so quickly?

Pretending to walk across the studio nonchalantly, Shanna sought her bottle of water and took a deep drink, then turned toward Kristoff. "Apparently, our plan wasn't good enough. We didn't catch anyone in the act of filming us, as we'd hoped. No one has sent me another blackmail disc or threatened me as a result of the whole thing." She shrugged. "I guess it was a waste of time."

But it didn't feel like a waste, given what he'd done next...

After the scene had ended, Alejandro had pressed a button to drop a partition between them and the audience. Shanna heard the watchers filing out, which filled her with a sense of both loss and relief.

Then Alejandro had turned her to face him and taken her into his arms. For a simple hug. He'd said not a word, asked for nothing else. Just held her, stroked her hair, for several moments. She hadn't had that in a long time. Years. Her father and brothers certainly never gave affection. And she had wanted it so bad.

She'd clenched her eyes shut, resisting an urge to crawl deeper into his embrace and cry for all the fear—and conversely, the bliss—soaking her body. In the aftermath of their sex, her emotions had tumbled, jumbled, whirled all around. Up was down, backward was forward; nothing made sense except holding onto him.

Somehow, she'd managed to restrain her tears, yank herself from his arms, and don her clothes.

Within minutes, Del emerged into the room with the unhappy news that security had been scouring the footage of the event and found no one in the audience with a camera of any kind.

After Del left, Shanna had lost it. Tears had fallen hard and fast. But silently. She didn't think Alejandro had noticed.

She'd been wrong.

He'd swooped her up into his arms. "Don't cry."

She'd been weak, and Alejandro had felt so strong when he'd settled her against his powerful body, in the shelter of his arms, and kissed his way down her face. He'd been so tender, as if he'd known exactly what she needed. He'd ripped right through her fragile barriers. She'd opened up to his whispered words and gentle mouth...

Then he'd taken her hand and led her out of the main house, down a pathway hidden by tropical plants and climbing ivy, softly lit by the full moon, then pushed his way toward a luxurious cottage.

His private quarters.

Being alone with him when she was so emotionally raw...not smart. Downright scary, in fact. Even the idea made her heart race, her palms sweat.

Clutching her keys, Shanna had mumbled something about a fictitious early-morning practice and fled.

The pain etched on Alejandro's face haunted her, but it was done. They were done. Now, she needed to get her mind off of the repeated messages he'd left since and focus on dancing. She had the biggest competition of her career to prepare for. He had a business to run. Why he continued to pursue her, she had no idea. They had nothing in common.

Except great sex.

"Earth to Shanna," Kristoff joked. "Are you with me?"

"Yes. Sorry. I have a headache." That wasn't a lie actually...just not the whole truth.

"Sorry. What should we do next about...the problem? Perhaps you should seek out a new partner."

He looked so sad at the prospect. Something in her chest twinged, and she shoved it aside.

"We don't have time to talk about this now. You have to be at work in two hours, and I have to meet with the costumer shortly. Let's focus on today."

"It would not hurt you to talk to me. Do you want to replace me? Do you want to talk about what happened at Sneak Peek?"

As her brothers would say, oh, hell no. "Talking will not win us any trophies. From the top."

Using the remote control, she started the music again and got into position. Sighing, Kristoff assumed his pose and they danced for another grueling half hour.

Until the door to the studio swung open unexpectedly.

Alejandro strolled into the studio looking dark and yummy and like a man with an agenda in mind—that started with getting her out of her clothes.

Shanna sucked in a breath. "What are you doing here?"

"I assume your phone is broken, since you have not returned my calls." He arched a brow. "So I decided to find you."

"We're practicing."

The protest was automatic. His presence here, so unexpected, raised her defenses. Thank God. She needed those barriers against him. Another hour with the man, feeling as weak as she had while he touched her, and she'd collapse against him and... *Shiver.* She'd admit that she cared. Be vulnerable to him.

Not on her agenda. In fact, it was totally unacceptable.

"You will win because we will discover exactly who has been blackmailing you," Alejandro vowed.

"The security tapes turned up nothing, you said."

"That is true. And I assume the blackmailer has not contacted you, or you would have let me know."

"Yes, I would have." And she would, no matter how much talking to him would have tempted her to do more...much like he was doing now. "But nothing so far. So we have nothing else to say."

Alejandro looked like he could see right through her bluster and wasn't put off in the least. Damn him! Why couldn't he cringe, like most people?

"How did you find out when and where we were practicing?" she demanded.

With a sweep of his hand, Alejandro outted Kristoff as the culprit.

She whirled on her partner angrily. "This is practice time, not social hour. What the hell were you thinking?"

"That if I did not tell him how to find you, he would end my privileges at Sneak Peek."

Shanna gritted her teeth. Fabulous. Yet another shining example of a man thinking with his penis. Apparently, it had never occurred to him—or he didn't care—that she had not wished for Alejandro to find her.

"I have been thinking," Kristoff said, "since your first effort to draw out the blackmailer did not solve the problem, you should try again."

"Try again?" Her jaw dropped.

Kristoff nodded. "Stage another public scene. The word about it is out now. People in the community are buzzing about you two. If you give advance warning, I believe the person responsible will come."

Shanna considered Kristoff's words with dread—and excitement. More of Alejandro's touches, his wild sort of lovemaking... So very tempting. She hadn't just liked what they'd done together; she had basked in it. And had been aching for more since.

No. More of Alejandro would only addict her further to the man. And while she didn't know him well, she doubted he would settle for a woman whose schedule was as demanding as hers. Someone who spent nearly every day dancing in very suggestive ways with another man. And Alejandro would expect a great deal emotionally of the woman he called his—certainly more than she was comfortable giving. He had to see her limitations.

So why was Alejandro pursuing her?

As much as she'd like to give in to her fears and dismiss Alejandro, what Kristoff said made sense. Maybe the blackmailer had not acted last time because he hadn't known about the scene. She and Alejandro had done nothing to spread the word beforehand. The audience who had witnessed her coming apart in his arms had all been there purely by chance.

"I agree," Alejandro said. "I want to catch this bastard. But the choice is Shanna's."

She bit her lip. With the competition in three days, her options were running thin. And throwing away more than fifteen years of training, sweating and suffering to avoid having sex with Alejandro seemed beyond stupid, even if something in her gut was telling her to run like hell.

Before she could overrule logic, Shanna nodded. "I'll be there tonight."

Alejandro shook his head. "Tomorrow night. Give me time to spread the suggestion that there may be a repeat performance, just in case the scum does not have his ear to the ground, so to speak."

Shanna released the breath she didn't realize she'd been holding. She wanted desperately to be with him. And, at the same time, she didn't. It was so unlike her to be indecisive and conflicted, damn it. She had to regain balance, regain control.

"Fine," she announced. "I will be there at eight. We'll commence at eight-thirty. I need to be home by ten."

Turning away with a dismissive whirl, she reached for the remote control, intent on starting the music, resuming practice...and ignoring Alejandro before he noticed her trembling and made her completely insane with those hungry stares of his.

Instead, he grabbed her arm and turned her to face him. "You will be there at eight-thirty. We will commence at nine. If it takes a whole night of public performances, you will stay until we know who and what we are dealing with."

She jerked from his grasp. "Don't presume to tell me what to do."

"Shanna, can you really afford to be impractical and put on your bitch armor with me?"

No.

"I know that is not you, and I seek only to help you," he murmured.

Still, she raised her chin, refusing to back down. "Whatever. If it amuses you to play the caveman—"

"No," he leaned into her and whispered for her ears only, "but it amuses me to see you hide from me and the absolute pleasure you know I am going to give you when I have you naked and under me again."

Hours later, Shanna had showered, changed, and run errands. Life was normal...and yet she was still both seething and uncertain about Alejandro's comments. Arrogant comments. How could the man manage to irritate and arouse her in a single sentence? For that matter, why did he always incite conflict inside her?

Argh! She needed to get him out of her mind.

Her doorbell rang. Oh, hell. She wasn't expecting anyone. Probably someone trying to sell her something. Maybe Girl Scout cookies. One of the neighbor girls had been selling them yesterday, and the thought of indulging in mindless sugar perked her up.

Shanna opened the door.

Someone stood on the other side, all right. It sure wasn't a Girl Scout.

"Alejandro." His name slipped out as a whisper.

"Good evening, *querida*."

When he called her that, she melted. Every time. "Don't call me that."

"Why does it bother you that I call you darling?"

"I am not your darling. We are working together to solve a common problem."

"Hmm. We are. But I fail to see how that must be the end of it."

Shanna opened her mouth to set him straight, but

Alejandro cut her off. "I am sure you will find some reason, but for now, let's not argue. I came to talk to you."

With narrowed eyes, she tried to gauge his sincerity. "Talk?"

"Nothing more."

She didn't quite believe him, but he had roused her curiosity. What could he possibly want to talk about with her?

"Come in." She stepped back to admit him.

Alejandro shook his head and held out his hand. "Come with me."

"Where?"

"It's a surprise."

"Not the club," she warned him.

"Not the club."

Now, against her better judgment, she was *really* curious.

Sliding into the sandals she kept by the door, she grabbed her purse and keys off the nearby table. "Will it take long?"

"Hot date tonight?"

His words mocked her. As if he knew that she could hardly wrap her mind around her interest in him, much less imagine being attracted to anyone else right now.

"With Dreamland, yes. I'm tired."

"And I am here to cheer you up." He held out his hand to her again.

This time she took it and let herself out the door. "Where are we going?"

"The nature of a surprise is that you should be surprised."

"You won't tell me?"

He shook his head, sending her a dazzling, unrepentant smile as they walked toward the condo complex's parking lot.

"You know that pisses me off."

"I know you are used to being in control and making all the decisions. A little relaxation will be good for you."

People had been saying that to her for years. Generally, she ignored them.

"That's your opinion."

"You cannot change it."

"Okay, but you're wrong."

"How about humoring me, then? Pretend."

She rolled her eyes. "Whatever."

Alejandro sliced her a little smile of victory, but wisely said nothing more.

When they reached the parking lot, he lifted his key fob and pressed a button. A red, late-model Mercedes convertible beeped and flashed its lights a few feet away.

Business at the club must be *very* good to afford the old place that housed their business and four-wheeled trinkets like this.

He assisted her into the car, then rounded the car to the driver's side, and eased in. "My father was a wealthy man."

"What?"

"I saw the way you looked at my car. I believe you had similar thoughts about the club. I am answering your unspoken question. My father was a wealthy man, and he left me his fortune."

"Not your mother?"

He shrugged and started the car. "I am the only part of him my mother will have anything to do with."

"They divorced?"

"In the Catholic church, no. They separated when I was

twelve." He backed out of the parking space and steered into the gorgeous summer night.

"Why are you telling me this?"

"You cannot like someone you do not know."

He wanted her to like him?

"My father was a philandering bastard, if you wished to know why they split up. I remember my mother's tears many nights when my father did not come home. They became my tears, too. He acted as if his affairs were both common practice and acceptable. Perhaps that was so in their generation... Perhaps it was accepted in his native Argentina..."

Alejandro was sharing something so shockingly private with her. Why?

"I do not agree," he stated. "If you speak vows and make a commitment, it should be solid. You should mean those words."

"True." Was he trying to tell her he'd be faithful? Why did he think it mattered to her?

The fact he wanted to make his opinion known unnerved her. But, being honest, it also thrilled her treacherous soft side. Having a man like Alejandro in her life full time would be wonderful...but distracting. Indulging was *not* an option. Their search for this blackmailing bastard and her need to win the California Dance Star consumed her every thought and waking moment. Her commitment was to winning. Romance would just interfere.

"Take my friendship with Del," he went on. "Del and I met in college. We quickly became friends—both outcasts to some degree, being foreign-exchange students with somewhat poor English here in Los Angeles. We discovered we shared a lot of similar interests and passions.

"So after graduation, we decided to put our degrees to work

on something mutually satisfying. Del used his marketing degree and social skills to spread word of the club and promote it all around. I used my finance degree to secure the funding, run the back end, invest our profits. We operate in the black, and each year is more profitable than the last. But two years ago, I had the opportunity to sell out my half for triple the amount I paid to get in." He shrugged. "Long ago, I promised Del I would stay in until we were both ready for a change. I declined the opportunity."

"That cost you a lot of money, I'm sure."

"Losing the friendship would have cost me more."

"You can afford to say that; you have your father's money."

"Not anymore. I put it in a trust for my mother. She thinks I set it up with my money. But the bastard owed her more than he could ever repay. I thought this was fitting."

Shanna stared at Alejandro as if seeing him for the first time. In a way, she was. It was hard not to like him when he was protecting his mother and defending his friendships.

A moment later, they stopped in front of a local ice cream shop, quaint and family-owned. In a few hours, after dinner, this place would be crawling with families. But during the dinner hour, it was nearly empty.

"Ice cream?"

"I assume you like it."

"I haven't eaten dinner yet. I was planning to cook before you came over…"

He climbed out of the car and helped her out. "Who needs dinner when there is ice cream?"

"Who doesn't need protein and nutrients? Ice cream isn't a dinner food."

Alejandro slipped an arm around her, and Shanna tried not

to melt against the tempting heat of his body. Why did he have to be so damn sexy?

"I will not tell your mother if you won't," he teased.

"My mother died when I was four."

She found herself choking out the words. She shouldn't have opened her mouth; it was only making her more vulnerable to him. But holding the truth after he'd confessed all about his parents seemed petty.

"I am sorry."

She hung her head. "I don't remember her. I have this...impression of what her laugh was like. I don't even know if it's accurate."

He squeezed her against his side as they approached the counter. "So your father raised you?"

"Along with my brothers. They are all athletes."

"Which is why you are so driven to win." It was a statement, not a question.

"Second place is nothing more than first loser. It's the family motto."

"Ah, this explains your drive to win." He turned to the teenager behind the counter. "A scoop of chocolate peanut butter and...raspberry amaretto. Shanna?"

"None for me. I have to fit into my costume—"

"She will have the same."

"I will not!"

"Then pick your favorite flavors."

"You're going to force me to eat ice cream?"

"I am going to help you take a moment away from ambition and enjoy life."

When was the last time she'd done that? Shanna thought

back through the weeks, which became months...and quickly turned into years. The realization stunned her.

She hesitated, then caved in. It was ice cream, not a commitment. Tomorrow, she had a grueling practice scheduled. She'd work the calories off.

"Chocolate chip cookie dough and French vanilla."

Alejandro paid as other teenagers behind the counter assembled their cones. In moments, they were licking on ice cream as the sun dropped closer to the horizon, with the California breeze stirring all around them.

After the first taste, Shanna moaned. "This is amazing."

He smiled. "I discovered this place a few years ago. It's part of my weekly ritual."

"Where do you put it?" She eyed his hard body, absolutely no stranger to his rippled abs.

"I make up for it with plenty of cardio and carrots the rest of the week. But life is meant to be lived, no?"

Had she ever really thought about it in that context? "I suppose so."

"You have been a very single-minded woman for many years. Dance has been your focus, your ambition."

"And my passion."

"No one watching you dance would deny that. You are very talented. You know this, right?"

She supposed. Yes, she could dance. When she watched footage of competition, she knew she held her own in a room full of talented dancers. For the past few years, she even believed she began to shine a bit brighter than them, because she practiced harder and wanted it more.

"I'm pleased with my performances."

"This ambition, does it make you happy?"

Happy? An odd question. She didn't enjoy being frustrated by the champion status she had not achieved yet. But she *would* be a champion. Once the trophy was in her hands, life would be very sweet, and the sacrifices she'd made along the way would have been worth it.

All she had to do was get dangerously close to the most tempting man she'd ever met in order to catch her blackmailer.

Still, his question unsettled her. She'd never thought of her life in a happy/unhappy context. It just was. Of course, questioning her life was too easy to do when she had a man like Alejandro in front of her, reminding her of everything she'd been missing.

"Why shouldn't it?" she asked.

"The way that ice cream cone is dripping and the fact I've rarely seen you smile, I suspect you have spent so much time dancing, you are out of practice when it comes to living."

Dancing was life for her. So what if she didn't eat a lot of ice cream? "What are you, Dr. Phil?"

"Just a man who would like to see you happy." He brushed tender fingertips across her cheek. "What is the worst thing that could happen if you do not win Saturday night? Or ever?"

Immediately, she wanted to reject the thought. But it was a fair question, one she'd asked herself during long nights when aching muscles, nagging injuries and loneliness had kept her awake.

"I don't know." She shook her head. "I can't let that happen. Failure is not an option."

"You cannot control what will happen."

Yeah, that's what worried her.

"So what happens if you never win?"

She hated to even think the answer. But to speak it seemed

unbearably personal, and yet Alejandro had poured out a part of his soul to her. He had not mocked her when she'd spoken of her mother, or the rest of the family, or the origins of her ambitions. She had no reason to hide from him...except that he kept slipping behind her emotional barriers and it scared the hell out of her.

Why couldn't she put distance between them? Why did she even care about his feelings? Normally, she had no problem with pushing people away, but Alejandro was...different.

"I would feel like a failure," she whispered.

"You would consider yourself a failure, even after everything you have achieved?"

"Probably. I know my family would think I'm a failure. I have one brother who has been the top decathlete in the world. One has played in the Super Bowl. My father has two gold medals. I can't compete."

"Who asked you to?"

"You'd have to understand my family. For years, my brothers have endlessly tormented me."

He shrugged. "The nature of men and their sisters. Their way of showing affection is to harass you. More manly that way."

It wasn't that simple, and she didn't know how to explain it. "Family aside, I couldn't give up dancing. I *want* to win, more than anything."

"I would not suggest you give up dance. I merely think you should take the floor to indulge your joy of dance, not to pursue a trophy. The journey is the treasure, not the prize at the end."

"Now you're a philosopher?"

Alejandro shook his head and placed a soft kiss against her ice-cream cold lips. "Just a man who wants to see you smile.

Will you?"

Shanna looked at Alejandro. He was so comfortable with himself. Somehow wiser than a man who ran a sex club should be. He made everything seem so easy. Even personal discussions, which she usually downright loathed, felt freakishly natural. No pressure. No scolding or telling her how to do things. No taunting her about her failures. Just a steady voice, a tender touch, with lots of insight.

Lovely...but none of that would put a trophy in her hand.

Shanna wrapped her fingers around his and smiled. "There. Are you happy?"

"I have seen more genuine smiles at a beauty pageant."

Sighing, Shanna sat back and licked at her cone. "Why does it matter to you if I'm happy or not?"

Alejandro paused, seeming to weigh his words. "You matter. I would hate to see you sacrifice everything for something that may never happen. I suspect you gave up high school frivolity, lasting friendships, and romance for a hunk of metal and a title."

He was right...and wrong. Being a champion was everything to her.

"This is why I don't date." She stood and glared down at him. "I don't expect you to understand. No one does."

He stood and met her glare. "You have ended more than one dance partnership to pursue winning over friendship. What has that gotten you except a bad reputation? Those partners invested in you, cared about you. You cast them aside."

"I had to! One was so injured, it was clear he was never coming back."

"Might he have tried harder to recover if he had a reason to and a partner waiting for him?"

Guilt sliced through her. Maybe. Likely not...but maybe. Curt had been a hard worker and possessed a drive to win. Last she'd heard, he was selling insurance.

"Martin dropped me in competition. I could not risk that happening again. I'd lost faith in his ability, and a couple without trust does not function well."

"The drop must have been painful, and I understand why you would not want an incapable partner. As you say, trust is essential. You spent nearly two years together, yet you never gave him a chance to rebuild it between you."

She rolled her eyes. "What are you, my dance pimp? And before you start in on Jonathan, that decision was mutual. He wanted to get married more than he wanted to dance."

Surprise flashed across his dark face. "Really? My mother will be happy to hear that. She hates you because you ran off her favorite."

Shanna sat again. "Ugh! Everyone thinks that. We...just knew it was time to move on, both of us."

Speculation crossed Ali's face, but he didn't ask if she'd slept with Jonathan. For that, she was grateful. "And now, you have issues with Kristoff. What will you do if we cannot find our blackmailer in time?"

Good question. She'd been putting the decision off about her partnership with Kristoff. This was her year to win; she couldn't imagine forfeiting. But... "If we don't succeed in fishing this blackmailer out, I won't have a choice. I like Kristoff. He's talented and has a great work ethic—"

"But you have no problem leaving him behind?"

"It's business."

"And you will not let anything or anyone stand in your way, will you?"

His soft question nearly crushed her with guilt. She shoved the feeling aside. Giving up over half her life and the chance to finally reach her dreams? "No."

Chapter Seven

Alejandro paced in the security room, watching the video feed from Sneak Peek's front door. He checked his watch. Eight-forty five. People were beginning to stream in, in greater numbers than usual for this time of night on a Thursday.

The word about his scene with Shanna was out. He and Del had seen to it personally, not using names, of course...but promising it would be special.

If Shanna showed up. And he wasn't sure; she was fifteen minutes late. Where the hell was she?

"You're going to wear out the carpet," Del teased.

Alejandro shot him a dark glare. "She's not coming."

"She'll be here. You said yourself the woman is prickly and contrary for the purpose of needling you. You admitted that she likes to control her situation, so it can't have been easy on her when you told her when to show up, what to wear...and nothing about what she could expect."

All of that was true, yet he'd had a larger purpose than being a controlling jackass. "I want Shanna to lean on me. I want her to know that she can trust me."

He wanted her to see what it felt like for someone to stand by her, even if she wasn't winning.

"You can't force her to figure that out."

"Normally, I would not try, but with Shanna..." He sighed and stared at the video monitors that showed no sign of her arrival. "If I cannot find some way now to encourage her to latch on to me, she will slip through my fingers."

Del shrugged. "Why does it matter? I mean, I agree that she will be helpful in finding the blackmailer, but we can flush out the asshole without her."

"She is not just business to me; she's personal."

"How personal?"

Interpretation: How deep were his feelings? There was the question that had been plaguing him all day. Shanna meant more to him than catching a scumbag blackmailer, more than an amazing lay, more than an intriguing woman. Analyzing how it had happened and why was pointless. It was what it was, and Alejandro always trusted his gut.

"I think I am in love."

"That was fast. Less than a week." Del arched a dark brow.

"More time will not change what I feel, except to make it deeper." He sighed, knowing he spoke the truth, even as he said the words. "She is strong and vulnerable, smart, adorably stubborn and in utter need of someone to love. How can I resist?" He flashed Del a self-deprecating smile.

"How, indeed? If you intend to resist, get your poker face on fast. She's here."

Alejandro whipped his gaze up to the bank of monitors and smiled.

"Aww. She's wearing a damn trench coat," Del groused.

Laughter bubbled up inside Alejandro. "Of course she is." Her little rebellion. "But I will bet she wore what I sent her underneath."

"I can't wait for this." Del rubbed his hands together.

With blood beating a burning path in his veins, Alejandro burst out of the security office and stalked toward the front door. Del followed close behind.

Alejandro intercepted Shanna two seconds after she walked in. "*Querida*, are you all right?"

As Shanna strode in, she lifted her lashes and sent him a skittish glance. "Fine. Why wouldn't I be?"

Her guarded tone set off alarm bells. So she was trying to push her armor back in place, put distance between them. Damn it. Perhaps he had pushed her too hard last night...or made her feel too guilty.

"When you did not arrive at eight-thirty, I grew concerned."

"No need."

He reached up to help her with her coat. She jerked away. "Don't. Just wait until..."

"We are on stage and I'm supposed to fuck you?"

She swallowed and sent him a shaky nod that seared his guts with panic. After tonight, she was going to turn around and walk out of his life—unless he thought fast.

"Is something wrong?" He gentled his expression.

She looked away. "This is business. You're doing what you need to do. So am I."

"Shanna, this is not merely a business dealing or 'just sex' to me. I want it to be more than that for you, too."

She shot him a deer-in-the-headlights stare. "Until Saturday, I have to focus on fixing my problem. You want me to dance for the joy of it, not for the trophy. I can't be joyful if I already know before I dance a step that I won't win."

Alejandro sighed. He'd hoped he'd gotten through to her during their ice cream date, at least in some small way. But he'd been deluding himself. She was determined to shut him out and focus on nothing but the prize.

How the hell could he persuade her to stay with him after tonight, when she would only view him as a distraction, a speed bump slowing her race to winning?

"Not to interrupt, kids," Del said, "But you need to make your way back to the room so you can get started. Showtime is in eight minutes."

Resisting the urge to rake a hand through his hair, Alejandro gnashed his teeth. He needed a minute to collect a few props and his thoughts.

"Can you show her to the room?" he asked his business partner. "I'll be there in five."

Alejandro didn't wait for the answer. He brushed past them, into the security corridor, and let the door slam behind him. Dread and anger crashed into the bottom of his stomach. Unless he acted fast, this could well be his last chance with this woman. He had three minutes to figure out how to soften her heart toward him, convince her he wasn't just out to save his business or get laid. Convince her they could be more than partners beyond tonight.

Miracle, anyone?

Del escorted Shanna through the club. She was aware of people all around her swaying and grinding to the jazzy/bluesy music. But her thoughts... Alejandro had the lock on those.

Last night and today, he'd acted like he cared. Why? She'd told him over and over this was business.

Yeah, did it feel like business when he was deep inside you, making you scream? Or when he fed you ice cream and did his best to understand you, to help you like a friend?

The man had her so confused. What should have been

nothing more than a temporary arrangement for the sake of ferreting out a mutual enemy—and okay, maybe a little mutual pleasure—had suddenly become very tangled. In the space of a few days, she'd come to think of Alejandro as a fixture in her life. The thought of that fixture being removed hurt.

Dangerous. How could she focus on the competition with everything hanging over her head if she had to add new and scary emotions for Alejandro to the mix?

"Follow me," Del said.

They crossed the dance floor and edged around a couple panting heatedly and letting their fingers do the walking. Del escorted Shanna into a long hallway. At the end, he held a door open.

One peek inside, and she sucked in a surprised gasp. This was out of a fantasy! Plush, like a pasha's palace. Rust, gold, bronze, with accents of black and crème. An enormous bed. Pillows everywhere.

The audience would be bigger in this room. And closer. The opportunity for someone to bring in a camera was huge.

"We've got the security angles covered," Del assured her before she even opened her mouth. "There are cameras all over this place. We've spent all day rigging it up. If someone tries to film you here, we'll nail him."

He eased closer. Shanna tensed. Truth be told, the man made her nervous. He was dark like Alejandro. Both men had a wide streak of bad boy. Alejandro was like a fire, hot and sometimes unpredictable, never quite tamed. But Del...he could be a very cool customer. He'd do everything on his terms, in his time, his way. And show zero emotion doing it.

Now, he gave off the vibes of a predator. Shanna swallowed and raised her chin as he sauntered closer.

"Can I take your coat?"

Feeling too vulnerable for her comfort, she unbelted the coat and stripped it off. The red corset underneath and the matching black thong, garters and stockings went way beyond suggestive. Being naked would make her feel more clothed.

Del whistled, looking her up and down, lingering on her breasts. "You look hot. Damn hot."

She cleared her throat. His hungry gaze eating her up when she'd last been on stage with Alejandro had turned her on. Being alone with him, having him this close, while he wore that ravenous expression...it was uncomfortable.

She shrugged to pass it off as casual. "A costume like any other."

"You and Ali got a thing going?"

Shanna looked up at him in shock. When this was over, it was unlikely they'd continue to see each other. They were from different worlds. Whatever they might have had would be another casualty of her ambition. It shouldn't bother her.

But something wretched and heavy that felt an awful lot like regret smothered her. Pain followed, but she shoved it down.

"No," she finally murmured.

Flashing her a hot smile, Del leaned in, invaded her personal space. "That's good news. Very good."

The rapacious way he watched her gave her major pause.

"When you and Ali are done here...maybe you and I could hook up?" He dragged a fingertip down her arm, leaving a scream of tingles behind.

Was he serious? Del imagined that, after having sex with his friend and business partner, she was just going to throw Alejandro over and hop in his bed instead? Not likely. "Get your hand off me."

"Why?" Del shrugged. "You said yourself that you and Ali don't have a thing going. You're a gorgeous woman. I've seen you in action, and you make me hard. I'll treat you right, make you scream. I hear you're good at switching partners. What do you say?"

He reached around her and slung his hand low on her hip, almost on her ass.

Fury erupted in Shanna's gut. She grabbed his wrist, squeezed his pressure point until he winced, then shoved his hand away from her backside.

"What the hell are you thinking? No, the better question is, which part of your body is doing the thinking for you. I'm pretty sure I know the answer." She cut a derisive glare in the vicinity of his crotch, then shot a quick glance to the door. Where was Ali?

"What's the problem, baby?" He moved in closer again.

Her temper flared. *Dirt bag!*

She lifted her foot and dug her stiletto into his toes. He swore, and she smiled. "I'm supposed to have sex with your friend in less than five minutes."

His voice was strained as he reached down to cradle his injured toe. "You don't get sentimental about your partners. And you said you weren't involved with Ali. If that's the case, why shouldn't I ask a gorgeous woman if she wants to hook up?"

Why, indeed? Del was attractive physically. She didn't think he'd be demanding of her time, or try to get into her head and question her commitment to winning. Del would never take her out for ice cream and try to be her friend. He didn't rip past the barriers around her heart with just a touch. He wouldn't press her for more than sex.

But if she disliked Alejandro for all those things, why

wasn't she eager to get down with his sinfully good-looking friend?

"Alejandro is your business partner and best friend."

"Yeah, but if you're not into him, that makes you fair game. C'mon."

Shanna was still processing Del's words when he grabbed her and crushed her body against his. His mouth swooped down, capturing hers. At the first swipe of his tongue against hers, she knew nothing but panic.

And pure rage.

Twisting until she could reposition her legs, she delivered a hard knee to his balls. He backed away instantly, clutching himself.

"What is your problem?"

"I'll tell you exactly what I've told Alejandro: I have the most important competition of my career to focus on. I intend to win, and anything else is just a distraction I don't need."

"And that's your only reason?"

Alejandro shoved the stage door open. It collided with the wall, echoing across the stage, as he strode inside. He had the distinct impression he'd interrupted something.

In the middle, Shanna stood wearing the corset, garters and thong he'd sent her—and looking every bit as drop-dead sexy as he'd known she would. Though his dick was already hard at the thought of being inside her, this outfit added to the red blood cell count below his waist.

The righteous anger on her face made him pause. Especially when he saw Del two feet away, hunched over, clutching his balls and glaring at her.

What the hell?

"She's got a mean knee."

"He's got the disposition of a man ho."

Anger crashed into Alejandro, as if he'd been driving a hundred miles an hour straight into a brick wall. "You made a move on her?"

"Yes!" Shanna shouted.

Del tried to stand up straight. "You said she had a habit of switching dance partners. I wondered if that extended to sex. She swore you two had nothing going. If that's true, why the hell did she kick me?"

Then his friend did something bizarre. He winked.

Alejandro frowned...until everything fell into place. Del had been testing her. If Shanna didn't care a thing about him, Alejandro knew she would have gone for Del. Women did—in droves. Shanna had been turned on by him watching her just days ago. Why not follow through?

He had this feeling that the only reason Shanna had kneed his pal was because she had more feelings than she wanted to admit—and not for Del.

Suddenly, Alejandro resisted the urge to smile. Hope curled in his belly, warmed his heart, made his dick even stiffer. He'd test his theory tonight.

"We have no time to argue. Let's get this party started. Del, let the crowd in. Security tells me they are lined up down the hallway. Shanna, turn around and put your hands behind your back."

With an okay signal, Del turned away and headed for the door.

No surprise, Shanna hesitated. She'd assumed he would be pissed at Del's pass. She'd assumed Alejandro would be possessive. If he hadn't known Del for years and known how his friend's mind worked, he would have been.

No, Alejandro was just going to enjoy the fireworks before he got to the bottom of whatever was in her heart. Del was just helping him along.

"Is there a problem?" he asked. "People will be filing in within seconds. We should be in position."

"Fine." She presented him with her back.

What a luscious view! Feminine shoulders tapered down into a narrow, red-corseted back. The black thong bisected a firm, creamy ass he'd fantasized about fucking. Those garters and black thigh-high stockings hugging the toned curves of her legs damn near had him on his knees.

And if he played his cards right, she would be all his.

Forcing his stare back to her wrists crossed at the small of her back, Alejandro grabbed them. With a snap of his wrist and two quick clicks, he had imprisoned her in handcuffs.

She whirled on him, murder in her eyes. "What the hell are you doing? Unlatch these! I didn't sign up for this. We didn't discuss—"

Alejandro cut off her tirade by covering her mouth with his. She struggled...for a moment. Then he swept inside her mouth, tunneled his hands in her hair, and kissed her as if his very life depended on it.

She melted.

With a gentle nip and a soothing kiss to cover the sting, he pulled back and whispered, "We have an audience."

Releasing her, Alejandro walked a half-circle around her and cozied up to her back, letting her feel the heat of his body and his thick erection. She gasped.

The curve of her neck beckoned, and he trailed his lips up

the graceful curve and soft skin.

Briefly, he opened his eyes and discovered at least twenty-five people in the room—and more filing in. Perfect. Maybe they'd catch the asshole tonight.

Then he put everything out of his mind except Shanna.

His hands started at her shoulders, but quickly developed a mind of their own. Down they plunged, right over the curves of her breasts pushed up by the tight corset. But having those nipples covered wasn't going to do.

In a few seconds, Alejandro brushed through the little buttons holding the garment together. It fell to the stage in a soft wisp of fabric.

Men groaned in the audience as he bared Shanna's breasts. She tensed. Alejandro could feel her shivering. Cold? He didn't think so. Nerves? Maybe. Excitement. Definitely. He could smell the beginnings of her arousal.

Standing behind her, he reached around and cupped her breasts in his hands, squeezing her nipples between his thumbs and fingers. Against him, she writhed, wriggling her ass against his cock. Hot shivers crashed through his bloodstream.

He was about to go out of his mind.

With a yank, he pulled the sheer thong from her body. Another collective groan rang from the audience. Guys shifted weight from one foot to another, adjusted themselves in their pants, sat forward in their chairs. Shanna began to pant.

Alejandro dragged his palms down her abdomen. He itched to feel the silk of her pussy, see just how wet she was.

Moments later, he had his answer. Hot damn! Wet, welcoming, lush. She might be able to lie about her feelings for him, but her body couldn't.

Now was the perfect time to start testing his theory...

A quick point at Del brought his friend to the stage. Shanna tensed again. This time, he didn't think it was due to excitement.

Before she could say a word, he whispered, "I want to watch your breasts be sucked. Del will help us out."

"No," she whimpered.

"You change partners all the time. Why does it matter?"

Del approached her and pressed his body close to Shanna's. Alejandro didn't say a word, just lifted her breasts up to him.

The smile Del sent her said that he was ready for scorching hot sex, just before he bent to her.

"It just matters," she whispered. "Please no."

Lifting dark eyes to Ali, Del waited for a cue.

Alejandro had what he wanted for now. He shook his head.

With a wry grin, Del contented himself by placing a chaste kiss on the curve of her breast. But to show he wasn't going to be dismissed, he took a seat on a nearby pillow and set a scorching stare her way.

In truth, Alejandro knew they had to play along, just in case their blackmailer was in the room. But he wanted nothing more than to get Shanna alone. *Soon*, he promised himself.

Turning her to face him, Alejandro watched her stage smile collapse. She looked at him with a mixture of hurt, anger and relief. Apparently, swapping partners did matter to her. And he sensed that the sooner he got her to admit that about dance, the sooner she'd settle into having one man in her life.

Impatient to touch her, Alejandro tore down the zipper of his leather pants and freed his stiff cock. "Suck me."

He kicked a pillow under her knees. Shanna hesitated, then sank down, her gaze on him the whole way, eyes bright with arousal and uncertainty. Then she bent her head and consumed him.

Oh, hell. Her mouth was a silken oven, soft and scorching and robbing him of breath. She damn sure knew what to do with that tongue of hers, caressing the length of his staff, curling it around the head. She sucked deep and hard, all the way to the back of her throat.

His heartbeat rattled in his chest. His ears buzzed with the excitement. Faintly, he was aware of male groans and a "fuck, yeah," from the audience. But focusing beyond Shanna's hot mouth was growing impossible.

As wonderful as it was, it had to stop. They had a show to put on for these guests—and a potential blackmailer. A blow job was all well and good but not blackmail-worthy, compared to Kristoff's show.

With a groan of regret, Alejandro cupped her cheeks and lifted her mouth from his cock. Then he helped her to her feet. In four steps, he had her bent over the huge, cushioned bed, her breasts pressed to the silk comforter. A few seconds later, he was sheathed and deep inside her.

She gripped him like no one ever had, like every contour had been formed just to clench around him. Tight.

He seized her hips and tunneled deeper. Then set a ruthless pace.

She cried out. The sight of her all spread out under him, her hands still cuffed at the small of her back, her pussy taking every inch he had...hell, he wasn't going to last long. And he didn't want to go off alone.

"I ache to play with your clit and feel you orgasm around me..." He hadn't even finished the sentence before he slid a pair of determined fingers right over the button of her nerves.

With his other hand, he gripped one of her hips. He thrust

inside her again and again, dragging the head of his cock right over that sensitive spot that had her muscles tensing, shaking.

In moments, a low, feminine groan split the air. Almost there...

"Come for me," he demanded. "Come!"

With another brush and press of his fingers over her clit, she screamed. Around them, the audience groaned. Several stroked their own cocks...even Del.

Then the rippling walls of her sex contracted, tightened, gripping and coaxing him, blotting out all other thoughts. Alejandro closed his eyes and focused on her. He shouted through clenched teeth as he followed her into ecstasy.

More than one groan of satisfaction split the air within moments. Alejandro didn't care. All he knew was that underneath him was the woman he would not let go of. They had seen to business.

Now it was time for the real pleasure—and hopefully, the future—to begin.

Chapter Eight

A pleasure cloud. Heavy limbs, light head. A gentle throb between her legs pulsing as it slowly abated. Alejandro's embrace providing warmth, even as he gripped her as if he'd never let go. Ah... Shanna could happily stay here, connected to him for a while. A long while. There were reasons she shouldn't, she knew. She just couldn't remember them.

Suddenly, Alejandro slipped free of her body and broke her sensual haze. She lifted weighty lids to watch him walk past her and snap the curtains shut between them and the audience. Del remained on their side of the drape, and Shanna was suddenly conscious of her nudity and Del's dark eyes on her.

"Keep them the hell out of here," Alejandro growled in low tones.

Del clapped his gaze on his buddy, who was now buttoning his pants. "You got it. Tomorrow?"

Alejandro smiled. "Maybe the day after."

What were they talking about? She should know, but her brain was so clouded by satisfaction, and thinking was just a lot of effort right now.

Del's laugh barely registered when Alejandro turned and stalked across the floor to her. In seconds, he uncuffed one of her wrists, grabbed her up in his arms, and headed for the stage door.

"What...? Where are you—?"

"Alone." He said the word like a vow. "No one except you and me, being us together."

Just in case others could hear, she whispered, "But the blackmailer—"

"If he was here tonight, he already got what he came for. Del will call me if they captured something on the security cameras. Now, this is about us."

"But you said we would stay all night, if necessary."

He stopped. "Is that what you want, for me to fuck you again for an audience? Shall we invite more people in this time?"

Sarcasm. Anger. And she understood. Something inside her rejected the notion of more audience time, too. "No."

"Good. I'm done sharing you with other hungry male eyes." He pushed through a door, out into a bright hall, past the open door to security. Laughing and clapping ensued from the crew inside the office, and Shanna buried her head in his neck.

"I'm naked!" she shrieked.

"They just watched us on the cameras. They are not seeing anything they have not yet seen. Which is another reason I want you all to myself."

Shanna didn't get another word out before Alejandro opened another door and let it slam behind him. Now it was dark, and Southern California's summer evening sky simmered all around them in a velvet hush. Frogs and crickets hummed in the sultry breeze. The lights of the city beyond the hill twinkled and winked as far as she could see.

"It's beautiful out here."

"The fact I would rather look at you should tell you how I feel about your beauty."

Shanna snapped her gaze up to Ali's. No smile. The weight of his stare was full of gravity—and rising need.

"Alejandro, maybe we should talk about—"

"No. Tonight is about you and me, no conversation, no people, no blackmail, no cameras. I need to feel you, like I have never needed anything before."

She gaped, totally unable to deny the breathless rush of joy at his words. Did he...care? About *her*?

There was no time to ponder the answer before he spirited her into his cottage, through the intimate cocoon of the hushed night, straight to his bed. In the shadows, she could make out its straight lines and modern flare. It was big, dark, exotic—just like the man.

Then the mattress was at her back, and he grabbed the empty cuff dangling from her wrist, and Shanna expected him to attach it to his bed somehow so he would have her at his mercy.

Instead, he attached the cuff to his own wrist.

They were joined. Together. Bound.

"Alejandro?"

He didn't answer her. Instead, he tossed the handcuff key somewhere on the floor, far out of reach, then covered her mouth with his own.

Shanna expected his ravenous hunger, the rapacious, hard-edged, *boom-fast-now* sort of touch. She was shocked instead by soft insistence. His kiss was seduction itself. Thorough, unhurried, deeper. Unabashedly intimate, as he conveyed his every want, spoke with his soul, communicating only with his mouth.

It was impossible not to fall under his spell.

A new ribbon of desire tied her stomach up in knots as he

trailed hot kisses across her cheek, down toward her neck. His exhalation felt hot against her neck, close to her ear, stirring sensitive skin. She shivered as his lips caressed her, branded her. He swept a fingertip down the arch of her throat and nipped at her lobe.

"*Necesito tocarle, su cara, su piel. Su corazón.*"

Shanna had no idea what his words meant, but they undid her. In that moment, whatever he wanted, she wanted, too.

"Tell me..."

He didn't right away. Instead, he swept his mouth over hers again. The tangle of breaths, lips, tongues became a deliberate kiss of endless hunger. Eloquent, shockingly sexual as the fingers of his free hand sifted into her hair, curling possessively around the strands. Toe-curlingly intimate as he tore his mouth from hers to stare, penetrating her with eyes like burning coals in the pitch of night. Ensnared, Shanna could not look away.

"I said that I need to touch you, your face, your skin. Your heart."

Something both shocked and joyous burst inside her. She gasped, and Alejandro swallowed the sound with another drugging kiss.

With every brush of his lips, every glide of his hot palm, every male moan poured into her mouth, he ripped past her barriers until she opened completely to him—parting her lips wider to accept more of his possession, clutching one hard shoulder with her free hand to keep him near, spreading her thighs apart to invite him inside. She sighed when his narrow hips fit right into the curve of her body as if he'd been born to be there.

"Yes." She arched under him, unable to hold anything back.

He fit his free hand under the curve in her back, keeping

her breasts and the damp heat of her skin right against him.

"*Yo le tocaré toda la noche. Cada parte de tú sabrás el se siente de mí.*"

"Ali...please."

The way he touched her, as if he had no other thought in his head except pleasing her... She burned inside her skin, yet she knew only he could save her. He would shatter her into a million pieces first, then remake her a new woman. A warning bell went off in some distant part of her mind, but his fingers gripped her hip, fitting her directly against the hard column of his erection. He wound down her body and brushed soft lips against the side of her breast.

"I *will* touch you all night long," he translated. "Every part of you will know the feel of me."

She had no doubt Alejandro would keep that promise.

He suckled her nipples over and over, lavishing attention on her until they stood red, swollen, so sensitive that nothing more than his breath on her induced a shiver. All the while, the fingers of his free hand whispered across her skin. Her back, her thighs, her buttocks. Even her knees, calves, and toes. Alejandro touched every inch of available skin, finally drawing her legs up high on his hips so he could toy with the sensitive underside of her knees.

Gently, he rode her clit with his erection. Not pushing or grinding. Not bruising. Instead, a soft nudge of delicious pressure in a hypnotic rhythm, one that took her higher and higher.

The kernel of pleasure under her clit mushroomed, swelled, ballooned. Shanna panted, trying to resist the searing pleasure for just another moment. She dug the fingers not bound by the cuff into the hard flesh of his back, pressing down his body, far down, until she gripped his ass in her hand.

Moonlight spilled past open blinds, swirling in on the evening breeze as he whispered, "*La piel estas rosácea, mi amor. Eres maduro y listo, sí?*"

"Tell me, Ali. Oh my... Yes!" She moaned.

"Your skin is rosy, my love. You are ripe and ready, yes?"

"Yes. Yes, now!"

He pressed against her again, nudging her clit with his cock. The cream of her arousal spread all over his flesh, and the next time he rocked against her, the bead of nerves he teased leaped at the slick pressure. Blood rushed south, pooled between her legs, jettisoning need, pleasure, and anticipation right where it impacted her most. Perspiration dampened her body. She clawed, cried in his arms.

"Who is here, Shanna? Who is in this room?"

"Us. Just us."

"*Apenas tú y mí. Ninguna audiencia. Ninguna cámaras. Nosotros,*" he breathed as he gathered the crooks of her knees into his arms. "Just you and me. No audience, no cameras. *Us.*"

The way we always should be. The thought ran through Shanna's mind unchecked, unchallenged, unstoppable as Alejandro paused, probed, then on a long glide, penetrated her.

His hard flesh filled her sex, sank deep, deeper, then deeper still. Making love face to face...totally different than being dominated by him for an audience. The slick rasp of his engorged shaft raked against her sensitive walls. A jolt of pleasure coiled, tightened, intensified, growing faster than she could assimilate.

"So tense, so tight, my love," he murmured as he drew back and brought their cuffed hands up to her breast. Her palm cupped her flesh as his thumb caressed her nipple. It was as if they were seeing to her pleasure together, and it drove Shanna straight to delirious need.

All the while, the slow steady pleasure of his thrusts turned her into a wild woman. She writhed, lifted her hips, arched—anything to reach more of him, lure him deeper still into her.

Alejandro went willingly, every lingering slide of his erection inside her lifting her arousal higher. Her pulse pounded in her ears. Heat suffused her body. She could barely breathe. And she didn't care.

For the first time in years—maybe in her life—she didn't just feel; she was wholly alive, driven by something more than her desire for a trophy of faux gold on her mantle. She lived for today, for now.

She lived to hear the man growling words in a language she didn't understand but adored as he strained, breathing harsh, to fulfill every promise of pleasure boiling in her body. Alejandro gripped the hand joined to his by the cuff and laced their fingers together. He squeezed her hand tight as their breaths merged, their cries mingled.

"Come for me," he whispered.

The request from his mouth became a demand from his body as he thrust straight into her core again.

Shanna splintered into a million pieces, blinded by the brilliant pleasure bursting inside her. In the next moment, he followed her into the white-hot rush of shattering pleasure. *Oh God, oh God!* He was all over her, everywhere...inside her. Shanna doubted she could wash his possession away with a mere shower. It seemed unlikely that time and distance would completely free her from him.

She feared she'd given a piece of herself to Alejandro she'd likely never get back—her heart.

Sated and exhausted, Shanna pulled up in the driveway of the house she'd been raised in. She and all of her siblings had moved out years ago. Dad had stayed in the rambling house alone. Why, she didn't know. The place was haunted by the ghost of her mother, always smiling, always dancing around the kitchen.

She should have gone to her apartment first. Showered, changed into her clothes, had a cup of coffee before coming here. If she had stayed in Ali's bed, he would have offered her all that and more. Instead, she'd pleaded the need to use the bathroom and persuaded him to unlock the cuffs joining them. She'd waited a few minutes, until she was sure he'd drifted back to sleep, then dressed in one of his shirts and a pair of long sweatpants, then sneaked out. Not that it mattered. Ali was with her, in her, in a way that had nothing to do with the fact they'd had unprotected sex and everything to do with the fact she cared far more about him than she should.

Leaving him alone in bed had felt as if she'd torn away a part of herself. That scared the hell out of her.

The chilly California air of the early morning hadn't helped to sort out her head. She was in love with a man who would never intend to stand in the way of her dance dreams. But how could Alejandro not, as consuming as he was? She'd barely driven two miles from Sneak Peek when she'd been hit by pain from the withdrawal from his warmth, his acceptance and tenderness.

Dangerous. She was the Bitch of the Ballroom because discipline and a ruthless dedication to perfection prevailed— and would win her that long-coveted trophy. When the music was high and the lights were on her, the judges didn't care what was deep in her heart. She'd do well to remember that.

Still, those moments in his arms... For the first time in years, maybe ever, she'd felt adored, and not because of what she might achieve or what competition she might win. She didn't have anything to prove in that moment. Alejandro cared about her. *And he shows it in amazing, creative, pleasure-drenched ways,* she thought to herself with a smile.

Then she realized she was wearing a sex-induced smile while standing in front of her dad's house on the day before the biggest competition of her career. Her smile faded.

She clutched a bag of bagels and cream cheese, along with a portable carafe of coffee she'd purchased at a bakery, and let herself into the house.

Shanna followed the smell of burned toast with a poignant smile.

She sauntered into the kitchen and looked at her father, older now, gray at the temples, his reading glasses askew, but still vital and well built for fifty-something.

"Bagels?" she offered.

Her dad plucked charred bread from the toaster with ginger fingertips, then dropped it on the counter with a curse.

Then he skewered her with a stare. "Sure. As soon as you explain why you're wearing a man's clothes, are rosy with whisker burn, and smell like sex."

Certainly nothing off about his sensory perception. She flushed. "I do things beyond work and practice at the dance studio."

"I never noticed it until today. You've always been very single-minded about winning."

"I still am. What happened last night won't happen again." She passed him the bag of bagels, hoping it would distract him.

He ignored the gesture and arched a sharp brow, as if he

disapproved. But Shanna couldn't shake the impression that he was suppressing a smile.

"I suspected it would happen someday. Maybe it's the female way. Who is he?"

Shanna frowned. "What do you mean, the female way?"

He shrugged. "Women follow their hearts, which usually lead them to some man or another, who may or may not respect their desire to keep pursuing their goals."

Exactly. No doubt, he'd have complete disrespect for her if she ultimately made that choice. Her brothers, too.

"Which is precisely why Alejandro and I are...done."

"Alejandro? Do I know him?"

Shanna shook her head. "Argentinean. He owns a nightclub. We met at the benefit for the Catholic orphans charity last weekend."

God, it was weird to be discussing her love life with her father in the kitchen of her childhood at seven in the morning. She needed coffee for this.

"Hmm." Her father hesitated. "What does he think of your dancing?"

"I assume he's okay with it. Not that it matters." Shanna sipped the caffeine-laden brew and let it sink into her hazy brain.

He reached for the carafe of coffee and poured a steaming mug. "A hindrance, is he? Resenting your practices?"

"No." Not unless she was avoiding him.

"Latin men are notoriously jealous. He can't handle your time with Kristoff and the way your partner has to touch you?"

Shanna had to laugh. "No, he knows way too much about Kristoff to be jealous."

"So you're just worried he'd be a general distraction?"

"He would. The other night, I was headed for a sensible dinner and an early evening to bed. Big day of practice the next morning, which is vital with the competition coming up. He came by and just assumed I'd go out for ice cream with him."

"Ice cream. That's a huge problem." Her father sipped his coffee, seemingly deep in thought.

Somehow, Shanna got the impression he was laughing silently at her.

"It is! I can't afford to blow off sleep and eat a gallon of ice cream to satisfy some...romantic notion of his.

"And then he tells me personal stuff, about his childhood and friendships. He blurts out his views that commitment is absolute and infidelity is inexcusable. Why tell me? The whole incident is taking up my thoughts that should be directed to the competition. It's tomorrow, and last night, he kept me up half the night..."

Realizing she'd nearly spilled the details of her sex life to her dad, Shanna flushed, then continued with a safer topic. "The man is just consuming. Him just *being* steals my attention and leads my thoughts astray. Every trick I've used in the past to ward off would-be Romeos doesn't work with him. He just doesn't give up and won't go away."

"And you're so tempted to let him into your life that it frightens you." It wasn't a question. He seemed to *know* that's exactly how she felt.

"How...?" She grappled to find the right words. "You know?"

"Your mother and I each had lives before we married. Did you know she was a prima ballerina?"

A prima ballerina? No clue. "I knew she liked to dance around the kitchen and she was graceful..."

But her mother had died years ago, shortly before Shanna turned five. In some ways, her mother was as great a mystery to her as she would be if Shanna had never met her.

"American Ballet Theater. She was set to star in the season's *Giselle*. To this day, I'll never know what she saw in a cocky weightlifter coming fresh off a gold medal high. I had to have been a complete ass. But she claimed to love me. God knows the sun rose and set on that woman, as far as I was concerned."

Shanna frowned, sensing that she would not like what came next.

"You married her and—"

"Encouraged her to stop dancing. Made sure I got her pregnant with your brother so she had to stay beside me. I was a hugely selfish bastard where her time and energy were concerned. If I could take it back somehow and let her take her rightful place on stage..."

Mouth gaping open, Shanna stared at her father. *This* was the man who had driven her for years. Nothing she'd ever done was ever good enough. Second place was first loser. Quitting was the professional equivalent of a noose.

"I don't understand."

"I know." He sighed heavily and sat on one of the little wooden chairs they'd had forever. "I pushed you and pushed you. I don't think I realized until just now that I did it because I wanted to make up for what I did to your mother. She never said that she regretted her decision. But I'd catch her every so often holding her toe shoes with a wistful look on her face. I suspect she always wondered what could have been. I didn't want you wondering, too."

Shock ricocheted through her. Her father had intentionally killed her mother's dance dream? And now regretted it like hell.

For years, he'd pushed Shanna. As a child, she'd wanted to follow one of her brothers into their sports, but he'd specifically signed her up for dance class after dance class. Now she knew why. But...

"You sound as if you're encouraging me to continue with Alejandro. Why change your mind now?"

He stirred his cooling coffee. "I don't think your mother really regretted her decision to leave dance and marry, but I regretted standing in her way. She...just seemed happy. Your mother used to have this certain smile when she was particularly happy. A little lopsided, with a dimple in her left cheek and a twinkle in her eye. Every time I saw that grin, I knew she was at peace with herself." Her father paused, looked up at her. "Until this morning, I'd never seen that smile on you. But there was a moment when you got out of your car. I was watching through the window. I saw that smile on your face. I'm guessing Alejandro put it there."

He had. When she pushed aside her tumult about tomorrow's competition, happiness sneaked in, again and again. The thought that, after last night, she might never see Alejandro again, gouged her with deep shards of pain. And it shouldn't. Their relationship had been short. Intense, yes, but nothing to build a lifetime on, right?

Why did she feel like she was wrong?

"He sounds like the kind of guy who wouldn't demand you give up your dream," her father said. "If he can make you happy and give you the freedom to pursue what you want professionally, why aren't you grabbing onto him with both hands?"

Her dad made that sound like a very good question. "With him as a distraction, I may never win."

"If you love him, then you lose at life without him."

"If I...divide my time, I won't be as dedicated. If I never become a champion, you won't think I'm weak?"

"Would it really matter if I did?"

Shanna paused. Thought. Alejandro's love or her dad's approval? No choice. "No. I'm an adult."

"You need a man's love more than your daddy's blessing."

She nodded. "Jason and Kyle would make fun of me if I chose to be with Alejandro."

Her dad rolled his eyes. "They'd make fun of you no matter what you did. They're convinced that's their prerogative as big brothers."

In spite of the weirdness of the conversation, Shanna laughed. "You think?"

The smile faded as something occurred to her. "I'm not sure matters with Alejandro are as simple as you think. Let's say I've played very hard to get. He may not be talking to me after I, um...sneaked out on him this morning."

"Why don't you send him tickets to tomorrow's competition? I bet he shows. I want to meet the man who managed to see beyond the Bitch of the Ballroom act."

"You're coming tomorrow?"

He reached across the table and squeezed her hand. "I wouldn't miss it for the world. Whether you're crowned champion of the ballroom or of Alejandro's heart, I'm proud no matter what."

Chapter Nine

Waiting in the darkened corner of the ballroom's dance floor, Shanna drew in a deep breath, smoothed her hair, straightened her sleeve, shifted her weight. And scanned the crowd—again.

Nothing.

"You must not fidget."

If she hadn't been so nervous, she would have laughed at Kristoff. Why not just tell her she shouldn't breathe? "I know. Sorry."

"You are nervous?" her partner hovered behind her and whispered in her ear. "Do you fear losing?"

The competition? No, not really. They would lose, and she'd accepted it. But Alejandro? Absolutely she feared losing him. In fact, she suspected it was already too late.

Shanna had delivered the tickets to Sneak Peak in person this morning. Del had greeted her at the door. Actually, greeted was a strong word. Met was more accurate. Reluctantly, in fact. His behavior had been considerably cooler than their last meeting. When he said he'd give the tickets to Ali, she added that she hoped he would visit her before the show so they could talk. Del had merely given her a terse nod, then shut the door in her face.

Clearly, she'd pissed Ali off enough to annoy the hell out of Del.

Alejandro hadn't come to see her before the competition. Another scan of the ballroom...there sat her father, who waved. She smiled back, but she still didn't see Alejandro's coffee-dark hair, swagger, or sin-laced smile.

Had she pushed him away one too many times? The painful thought tightened her stomach into impossible knots. Throwing up didn't feel out of the question.

"Shanna, you are nervous about the routine?"

No. She and Kristoff were ready. Beyond ready. They knew these dances. They had perfected their chemistry and rhythm on the floor. The blackmailer's DVD would keep them from winning, but they would give their best showing.

"Or do you regret that you were unable to replace me with a new partner in time for this competition?"

Scowling at his bitter tone, Shanna glanced over her shoulder at Kristoff. Mouth pinched, eyes tight, shoulders stiff. Damn, he looked nervous. Petrified. What was that about? He was never wound up before a competition. Maybe he was rattled about the DVD circulating the judges' table?

As Kristoff continued to watch her with narrow, burning eyes, and she replayed his question in her head, Shanna finally understood.

"I'm not replacing you." She dropped her arm to her side and reached for his hand, hovering near her hip. She gave it a friendly squeeze. "I never auditioned anyone else. You were right about the partner swapping; it was stupid."

He shot her a suspicious stare. "Why the change?"

"I used to bury my guilt about dropping someone for the sake of winning. It never worked. You made me see how pointless it was." *With a little help from Ali and Del.*

"You do not seek to replace me? Truly?"

She smiled. "You're stuck with me."

Kristoff leveled his mega-watt smile at her. "For weeks, I cannot stop from worrying you plan to replace me." He squeezed her hand. "Thank you. I am happy now."

"We win or lose together, okay? Besides, maybe we haven't been winning because we've forgotten that dancing isn't all serious. Maybe...we just need to have fun with it tonight, see what happens."

Kristoff hesitated, then teased, "Who are you and what have you done with my partner?"

Despite her nerves and her worries about losing Ali, Shanna had to laugh. If nothing else, she'd cemented one important relationship tonight. And damn if it didn't feel good.

"If we were alone, I'd slug you for that."

"There is the Shanna I know and adore," Kristoff muttered.

Just then, the music ended, and the announcer reminded the crowd of their competitors' names and number. Shanna drew in a relaxing breath. *In. Out.* They were next.

"Before we go on, I must tell you something."

"Kristoff, we're about to be announced."

"This is true, but—"

"Couple number one hundred three, Shanna York and Kristoff Palavin from Los Angeles, California."

The crowd cheer wasn't as enthusiastic as Kristoff would like, Shanna knew. She should care, she supposed, but right now, she couldn't get past the fact that Alejandro had chosen not to use the tickets she'd left him.

Which meant he'd given up on her, she feared for good.

Forcing a smile as the onlookers clapped, she walked onto the dance floor, Kristoff beside her, cradling her palm in his. They struck their pose and waited.

Doing her best to focus on the next three minutes, Shanna plastered on a smile and projected it to the crowd. The music burst over the quiet, Shanna arched, kicked, and turned.

There sat Alejandro.

His face gave away nothing, but the grin that shaped her mouth was her first real one of the day.

He's here. Here!

And he looked incredible in a black suit, white shirt and a satiny charcoal tie.

She knew he looked even better out of the suit.

Before she whirled around to face Kristoff again, she flashed Ali a look she hoped communicated just how thrilled she was that he'd come.

Over the next two minutes, forty seconds, she and Kristoff poured their souls into the dance. And he was spectacular, as if some light had been turned on inside him. Relaxed yet crisp. Strong. God, he played to the crowd. He really was incredible. Shanna responded, acting the part of the seductive female to his commanding male in the tango.

No doubt in her mind, they sparkled, shined, brought the *WOW* to the dance floor. Shanna couldn't remember the last time she'd enjoyed dancing so much.

When the music ended, she knew they had done their best. *Knew it.* Yes, she'd love to win tonight, but if it wasn't in the cards, they would spend a year living down the scandal and practicing their butts off. They would conquer this trophy next season.

The crowd stood, cheered, their enthusiasm catching.

Never before had she felt so liked by the crowd, so connected to them as she and Kristoff bowed.

She turned her head slightly to see Alejandro. He, too, stood and clapped, then bent to whisper into the ear of a small but striking middle-aged woman who shared his eyes. His mother.

Then he turned his attention back to her, fixing burning hazel eyes on her, and Shanna felt the zing and sizzle all the way to her toes.

Damn, she loved that man.

"You and Alejandro?" Kristoff asked as they left the dance floor. "You have a...thing?"

"What?"

"You looked at him as if you cannot wait to devour him, as if you are all his. Or as if he is all yours. Is that so?"

Shanna swallowed a lump of nerves. God, she hoped Alejandro's being here meant that he'd forgiven her for running away and not believing in them... If not, she wasn't giving up. No more switching partners for her when things got difficult— not professionally or personally.

"That's my plan."

"In fourth place..." the announcer droned, and Shanna listened long enough to realize her name hadn't been announced, then clapped politely.

This was usually the part of the event that made her most nervous. How many times had she stood at the corner of the stage, trying not to pass out, praying she would not be disappointed by failing to grab the trophy again, only to hear her name announced long before the first place winner's? How many times had she trotted out her plastic smile, like third place thrilled her, while feeling crushed inside? Too many.

But tonight...she almost *wanted* the announcer to call her name now, so she could finish this dog and pony show and talk to Alejandro. His face still gave away absolutely nothing, not anger, not joy. Had he forgiven her and come to be with her? Or had he simply come because she'd given him free tickets and his mother liked to attend? No clue. That man could probably play a mean game of poker.

"In third place..."

Again, not her name. Another polite clap. Another clandestine glance at Alejandro. He raised a brow at her, but his expression remained utterly, frustratingly unreadable. Forget the contest results. Not knowing how Ali felt about her was killing her.

And what did that say about how much she loved him? She was well and truly hooked.

"In second place..."

Not her name again. The couple beside them swept out on the floor, and Shanna could see the woman's forced smile hiding disappointment and the crushing blow of defeat.

But wait...if second place had been announced, and there were no other couples out on the floor...

"In first place, the U.S. Latin dance ballroom champions, couple one hundred three, Shanna York and Kristoff Palavin of Los Angeles, California!"

Kristoff squeezed her hand as he led her out onto the floor. "We did it! We did it!"

They had. Finally! Alejandro was clapping for her. His mother, too. The whole crowd did, including her father, who enthusiastically whistled like he was at a football game. It was bad form in ballroom, but she smiled, glowed and grinned from ear to ear.

Tonight, she was finally a champion.

But how had it happened, given the blackmailer's threats?

"What about...you know?" she said to Kristoff through her smile. Maybe the threatening bastard hadn't followed through?

Before he could answer, the emcee came forward with their trophy. Kristoff grabbed it with one hand and hoisted it up in the air, along with their joined hands. Together, they bowed.

Professionally, she had never been happier than in that moment.

"Ms. York and Mr. Palavin are now eligible to compete in the upcoming World Dance Cup Latin competition."

Wow, a huge dream come true. And yet... Her world would be flawed, her triumph hollow, if she didn't have Alejandro to share it with.

The emcee took the trophy from Kristoff. The lights dimmed, and as champions, she and Kristoff danced. But her mind was on Ali, the way he watched her, his face shuttered but his posture relaxed. What was the man thinking?

Soon, others crowded onto the floor. With the spotlight no longer on them, Shanna all but forced him to tango Alejandro's way.

Kristoff resisted. "I must tell you something."

"Later. I promise."

"But—"

"Give me fifteen minutes, okay?"

Before he could reply, they reached the edge of the dance floor. She turned to Alejandro's mother.

"Mrs. Diaz? Hi, I'm Shanna York." She held out her hand.

"*Ella es su novia?*" his mother asked Alejandro sharply.

"*Mamá...*" He sighed. "*Sí.*" Then he whispered something in her ear...and her entire face changed, lightened, glowed.

She turned to Shanna with a beaming smile and said in accented English. "Thank you for the tickets. Congratulations on winning, *nuera.*"

Nuera? Damn she was going to have to learn to speak Spanish at the first opportunity. "Thank you. Have you had the pleasure of dancing with my partner, Kristoff?"

She shook her head and risked a shy peek at Kristoff. "He is one of my favorites."

"I'm sure he'd consider it a favor. He gets tired of dancing with me and would love your company." Shanna turned to her partner. "Kristoff?"

Her partner smiled charmingly and took hold of the older woman's hand. "Shall we dance?"

Off they went. Shanna watched Kristoff handle Ali's mother with aplomb as he led her into a waltz. The problem was, with Kristoff engaged, well-wishers and competitors were headed her way.

Shanna grabbed Alejandro's hand and dragged him backstage, down a poorly lit, winding hallway, into an empty office. She had no idea who it belonged to—and didn't care—but she shut the door behind her and locked it.

"Hi." She smiled. "You came. Thank you."

God, could he hear her heart pounding like a hip-hop song at full blast?

"You sent tickets. This competition meant a great deal to you." Shanna heard the edge of anger in his voice, glimpsed it in his tight jaw.

"Not as much as I thought. I know that now, thanks to

you." She bit her lip, wondering how bad it was going to hurt if he didn't want to hear what she had to say. "I'm sorry about...the other morning. You know, leaving you alone. For everything. Please tell me you don't hate me."

"I don't hate you."

His face still gave her no inkling about his true feelings, but Shanna considered his not hating her a great start. She rushed to Alejandro, threw her arms around his neck, and kissed him like there was no tomorrow.

Then again, unless she convinced him of her sincerity, there might not be a tomorrow for the two of them.

He kissed back. Oh, did he ever. And he tasted *so* good. Like brandy and a hint of cinnamon. Hot. And a few moments later, hungry, insistent as his mouth devoured hers. He threw his arms around her, banded them tight around her middle, as if telling her without words that she wasn't going anywhere again. She melted, might as well have become a puddle at his feet.

Long minutes and a pair of damp panties later, she broke away, breathing like she'd run a marathon. And unable to restrain a hopeful smile. "Does that mean you forgive me?"

"For leaving me alone in my own bed? Hmm, I may need more...persuading." A smile toyed at the corners of his lips.

"Does tonight work for you?" She cupped his cheek in her hand, looked right into those killer eyes, and threw caution to the wind.

"I may require more nights. Many of them."

Hope burst in her heart, so explosive, she could hardly breathe. "Ali, I am so sorry. What I did was insensitive. I know it. I knew then. I was just...scared. But I'm not anymore. And I want you to know that I care about you. A lot."

"Care." He quirked a dark brow. "In what way?"

Shanna knew she had his attention. Not only did she feel it against her hip, she felt it in his gaze, in the way his arms tightened around her.

"How much, *querida?*" he prompted again.

She swallowed down the tangle of anxiety and need and anticipation threatening to kill her courage. "I love you."

Those three words had barely cleared her lips before Ali stepped around her and, with an impatient arm, wiped every piece of paper off the flat, faux-wood desk and onto the floor. A moment later, her back was against the cool laminated surface and every inch of his body covered her completely, from the bunching shoulders beneath his elegant coat, to the hard abs that rippled with every breath, to the narrow hips...with the impressive erection between.

"Say it again." His voice was thick with demand.

"I love you."

"And you mean this?"

Shanna let her gaze delve straight into Alejandro's hazel eyes and she didn't look away. "Except to my dad, I've never said those three words to a man. Ever."

Finally, expression warmed Alejandro's strong, square face. Happiness, hunger, adoration...love.

"*Te amo, querida.*" He dipped his head for a long, sweet kiss. "I love you, too."

Then he kissed her again, long endless moments where Shanna felt blissfully lost in passion and joy. Alejandro's endless caress shimmered want in every crevice, corner, and nerve ending. She wanted the moment to last forever.

With a moan, he lifted his head, his hazel eyes snapping with a hunger like she'd never seen. "What I wish to do to you...with you, to show you how I feel..." He groaned, gathering her thigh in his grip, lifting it high over his hip, and grinding against her, right where she wanted him most.

Anchoring her hands in his short, inky hair, she planted her mouth against his and devoured him in turn with another kiss that sizzled her insides and rubbed her restraint raw. "Oh...I want to touch you, feel every inch..."

"That can be arranged." He dragged his palms up her back, down her sides. "How do I get you out of this infernal costume so I can make love to you?"

"I'm sewn into it."

"Damn it," he muttered, still feeling his way around her back. He followed that with a curse in Spanish that sounded melodious but was, no doubt, foul. Alejandro grabbed the neckline of the spangle-ridden dress.

"Ali—"

Shanna only got the first syllable out before he ripped the costume in two and pulled the fragments wide. Cool air hit her bare, overheated skin. Her nipples beaded at the sudden chill, then tightened again when Ali fixed his hot gaze on the rosy peaks.

"Oops." He sent her a slow, wicked smile.

She should be concerned about the costume. And she would be...much later. At the moment, she arched to him, silently begging for his touch. "These silly costumes are so fragile."

"Indeed." He shifted against her, pressing, his cock harder than ever as he palmed her breast. "If I had known you were nearly naked under there, I would have ripped the damn dress off the minute we cleared the door."

Stifling the explanation about undergarments being built

in, Shanna focused instead on the need tightening in her belly...and lower, where her flesh melted, swelled, slickened. Ached like she'd never been satisfied.

She laughed, but pointed out, "I have nothing else to wear. How will I get out of the ballroom without flashing everyone?"

"I will think of something," he breathed and nibbled a very determined path down her neck. "Right now, your wardrobe is not my top priority."

He latched onto one nipple with those full lips, his tongue providing sensual torture that made her arch against him and struggle for a good breath. Beneath him, Shanna wrapped her legs around his hips and writhed.

"Making you scream is," he clarified.

He backed away long enough to tear at her pantyhose, making them a candidate for the trash can, then he was back, hot and single-minded, his face feral. He reached between them, his fingers impatiently tugging on his zipper—and brushing her clit.

God, her temperature was rising, so fast, so high. Ali was an inferno in her blood, and she feared she'd never get enough.

A moment later, his pants fell past his knees. In the next instant, he thrust deep, pressing her harder onto the desktop and filling every bit of her with his cock. His gaze locked onto hers and never wavered as he withdrew almost completely, then glided back inside her, all full of seduction and friction so dazzling, her body felt like one big firecracker. The last inch of his erection he shoved inside her, startling her with a spike of pleasure as he rubbed right against her cervix, against sensitive tissues clamoring for more.

She gasped at the delicious coil of want gathering between her legs and closed her eyes. Being with Ali was like making love with a tornado. Wild, unpredictable, always strong and tumultuous. Constantly amazing.

"Look at me." His voice was hoarse, raspy as he pulled back and plunged deep again. "Mine."

His possessive streak shot her with thrill. He was definitely on the caveman side, and she loved it.

"Yes," she assured as she met his next thrust, hips rising, fingers clutching his biceps, which bulged with effort as he pushed deep again. "And you're mine."

"Let me show you how much." He gathered her legs in his arms and warned, "Hold tight. This will be a wild ride."

Excitement spiked deep, striking right behind her clit as he hammered inside her once, twice... God, at a pace so relentless, the orgasm that had been dancing just out of her reach, teasing her since he'd touched her, now loomed, pooling, converging, until the pleasure bubbled out of control, exploding with mega force. It drowned her completely.

Ali smothered her cry with his fervent kiss as he followed her over the edge, his body stiffening, shuddering, against her for long moments...then sinking deep against her, as if he'd found home.

At first, he didn't move, just peppered her face with adoring kisses.

Shanna wondered if she'd ever been happier. But she knew she hadn't. Suddenly, she had it all—the trophy, the man...the sense of peace she'd been wanting for years.

"I'm crushing you." Ali sighed with regret and started to rise.

"What a way to go." She smiled. "You know, I really don't have anything to wear out of here."

He smiled, sharp, greedy, just like she imagined a pirate would. "Hmm. I could happily keep you naked."

"And I would stay that way willingly if you'd keep having your wicked way with me, but, um...we have to get out of here first."

Ali glanced around at the utilitarian office. "Agreed."

Suddenly, he pulled away, zipped his pants, and prowled to a dark corner of the office. He grabbed a trench coat off the rack and turned to face her with a triumphant smile.

He tossed the coat her way. "Shall we get out of here, find someplace private?"

With a giddy laugh, she wrapped the coat around her and shoved the remnants of her costume in the trash. "With pleasure."

She barely had the sash belted around her waist when Ali pressed her back against the desk. Oh, my. No mistaking the fact he was ready for round two.

"Good. We're leaving. Now. You will come to my bungalow and stay all night?"

"Yes." And the next, and the one after, and the one after that, if he'd have her.

"You will not leave?"

"In the morning? No."

"Ever?"

Was he saying... "Are you asking me to...move in with you?"

He clenched his jaw. "No."

Her stomach plummeted. "Of course not. I misunderstood."

"My *mamá*, she would be very disappointed if we lived together. Just before you sent her to dance with Kristoff, a brilliant move, by the way, she asked if you were my girlfriend."

"You said yes." A smile crept across her mouth.

"I did, then I whispered in her ear. Do you recall?"

"Yes, what did you say? And what is a *nuera*?"

"I told her I had other plans." Alejandro kissed her neck, her cheek, working his way softly to her mouth, then whispered, "*Nuera* means daughter-in-law." He took a little black box from his pocket. "Interested in the role?"

"You're proposing?"

"Yes."

"Aren't you supposed to be down on one knee?" she teased.

"I would rather be on top of you, always. Will you marry me?"

"*YES!*" She clutched Ali tight as he opened the box. She fell in love all over again. "Yes!"

"Good. I wasn't taking no for an answer."

"It's beautiful," she breathed as he stood up and slipped the square solitaire on her ring finger. Tears gathered in the corners of her eyes, slid down her cheeks. Probably ruining her mascara—and she didn't care. "When did you buy this?"

His cheeks flushed a dull red. "About four hours ago. But I have known that I love you for far longer than that."

"Me, too. I was just too afraid that love meant giving up my dream. I'm sorry. Never again."

"Together, we can face anything. Shall we tell my mother and your father?"

"Yes. Just... I want another moment alone with you." She squeezed his hand. "This is the happiest night of my life! The win, the engagement... Wow, almost too much good stuff to take in. I feel so complete."

He brought her against him for an intimate hug. "Me, too. I'll be here to share your triumphs for the rest of our lives. But..." he frowned. "What happened to the blackmailer? He threatened to circulate Kristoff's DVD to the judges to prevent you from competing and winning."

"I know. I've been scratching my head, too. Maybe he changed his mind?"

A pounding on the door interrupted their closeness and musings. Oops...someone wanted their office back, and they'd made an absolute mess.

Shanna wiped away the mascara from beneath her eyes as Ali opened the door with an apology on his lips. "We are very sorry..."

But instead of an event manager standing on the other side, it was Kristoff.

"What?" Shanna asked. "Is something wrong?"

"I must talk to you."

She'd promised to talk to him in fifteen minutes. She supposed those were up. "Okay."

Kristoff paced; he looked oddly hesitant. "You are happy we won, yes?"

"Of course! Aren't you?"

He nodded. "Very."

"I don't know how, given the DVD and the threat but—"

"I did that."

"Did what?"

Grimacing, he confessed, "I created the DVD." He risked a glance at Ali. "Before you force me from Sneak Peek...I will tell you that the people in the video consented to be filmed. They are my...how should I say, boyfriend and girlfriend. We are together, and they agreed to help me."

Shanna had no idea Kristoff was in any sort of relationship, much less with both a man and a woman. Whatever floated his boat, but... "You're telling me you filmed the DVD and left it for me with the blackmailing note? *You* staged this? Why they hell... I worried until I was sure I had no stomach left for days!"

"This, I know. I apologize. But, um... before I invest many months and years in being your partner, I must know if you will stay with me. If I pretended like the news of my...relationship reached the judges, I wondered what would you do, keep me or dump me."

"So the blackmail...it wasn't real?"

"No. Do not hate me." His pleading expression tore at her heart.

A moment of anger surged through her...then died. He would never have needed to test her if she hadn't spent years partner-swapping to feed an ambition that, in the long run, had nearly eaten her spirit and happiness alive.

"I don't. Just don't, um...surprise me again."

"Now I know where I stand, so...never." He grabbed her left hand, noted the ring there, and grabbed her in a bear hug. "Engaged?"

She nodded, her smile off the charts. "Just now."

"Congratulations! You are happy, yes?"

"Incredibly so." She sent Ali a warm smile, and he caressed her back in return.

"I think all will be good now," Kristoff pronounced.

"Not just good." Ali brought her closer to his side, and she rested her head on his shoulder. "It's going to be perfect."

"Are you sure?" Alejandro teased.

"I'm a champion with a great dance partner and a wonderfully hot fiancé. I'm going to grab happiness with both hands and run."

"Really?" Alejandro challenged.

Shanna sent him a saucy smile. "You bet. Don't believe me? Just watch me."

"Oh, I will." He kissed her. "With pleasure."

About the Author

To learn more about Shelley Bradley, please visit www.shelleybradley.com or www.myspace.com/shelleybradley. Send an email to Shelley at shelley@shelleybradley.com or join her newsletter via the link from her website to hear more about new and upcoming titles.

Look for these titles by
Shelley Bradley

Now Available:

Naught Little Secret
The Lady and the Dragon
A Perfect Match

Show Me

Jaci Burton

Dedication

To my friend and critique partner Shelley Bradley, who slaps me good and hard when I need it. Thanks babe.

To Shan, who appreciates a good restaurant scene. Heh.

To Angie and Crissy. Thank you for this.

And as always, to Charlie, for the constant inspiration. Love you.

Chapter One

"Quit fidgeting," Melinda said, tapping at Janine's hand.

"I wasn't fidgeting." Janine removed her fingers from the hem of her skirt and clasped her hands together. "I would like to know where we're going."

"Someplace fun." Susan batted her lashes in a very mysterious way. "A place for you to unwind, let your hair down. You are going to *love* this."

Terri and Melinda exchanged winks, which was never a good sign. Her friends were always the mischief makers, while Janine had been the stand-in-the–background-and-out-of-harm's-way part of the foursome. She'd known better than to get involved in their wild and crazy schemes. If there was trouble to be found, they could find it, and Janine wanted no part of fun and games that could lead to scandal. She had too much to lose.

Especially now, when everything she did was under such tight scrutiny.

Janine Bartolino had turned thirty today, and her girlfriends were bound and determined to see that she celebrated in a major way. Though she much preferred a nice dinner at one of her favorite trendy Los Angeles restaurants, then back to her place for cocktails, the girls weren't having any of that. Susan, Terri and Melinda said they had a surprise for her. They were taking her out tonight for something special.

She hated surprises.

They'd had dinner at a nice restaurant, which had been , quite enjoyable. She never saw enough of her friends, so getting together was always a treat. She'd known them since college, and though they tried to get together often, they were all busy with their careers, so trying to plan an outing at a time when everyone was available was a lesson in frustration.

They'd managed to clear their schedules for her birthday, though, and she was grateful for that. She loved catching up. But she was nervous about tonight. What in the world did they have planned?

They'd shocked the hell out of her by picking her up in a limo—a true slice of heaven, there. The champagne had been flowing freely since seven o'clock that night. Good thing she'd eaten a decent dinner or she'd be toast by now. Champagne went to her head fast, the bubbles tickled her nose, and she was already dizzy.

"Almost there. Breathe, Janine."

She resisted the urge to stick out her tongue at Terri. Too juvenile. And she was thirty now.

Thirty. Ugh. It seemed old. She *felt* old. And so tired of all the responsibility heaped onto her shoulders. Maybe she should take her friends' advice and relax a little, just kick back and not worry what everyone thought.

Yeah, right. Like that was going to happen.

She'd been so preoccupied with her own thoughts, she hadn't noticed the limo heading into the Hollywood Hills.

"Where are we going?"

"You already asked that question," Susan said. "A hundred times or more."

Janine rolled her eyes. "You're exaggerating. I did not."

"Fifty times, then. Quit asking. We're not telling. But trust us, you're going to love this."

She highly doubted it. While she enjoyed getting together with the girls to catch up, they didn't run in the same social circles at all. Susan was a writer, Terri an actress and Melinda a model. They were all gorgeous, well-dressed and comfortable in their own skin.

Janine was...she didn't know what she was.

Other than thirty.

Quit reminding yourself.

She was also independently wealthy. And in charge of her family's fortune, with a ton of responsibility weighing on her head.

"Almost there," Terri said. "Look out the window. You can see the house now."

Janine leaned forward. House? They were going to a house?

Whose house?

It was amazing, looming up out of the hillside, all white in a sea of green. The limo pulled up in front of the well lit two story. The house screamed class and sophistication, instantly transporting Janine to another era. Subtle lighting showcased the place perfectly, from the gleaming stucco walls to the red bougainvillea draping over the porch.

"Okay, where the hell are we?"

The driver opened their door. "You'll see," Melinda said, tossing an enigmatic smile over her shoulder. She slid one elegant leg out the door. "Come on."

If this was some kind of surprise party, she was going to be really irritated. She'd made it clear she wanted nothing of the sort. The girls had promised. But since the others had already piled out of the limo, she had no choice but to follow suit.

They'd made her dress up, and not in going-out-to-dinner clothes, either, but in a slinky cocktail dress that hugged her body way too intimately for her own comfort. Black, skintight and revealing a dangerous amount of cleavage, Janine felt underdressed and overexposed. Of course her friends were dressed similarly, not that it bothered any of them in the least. Then again, they had the bodies for it. Janine always carried that extra five pounds she couldn't seem to get rid of, while the others were tabloid-magazine ready for whatever paparazzi happened to be lurking.

Though she didn't spy any cameras. In fact, no one was out front. It was quiet, the only sounds those of their heels clacking on the walkway and a waterfall in the distance.

As they approached the front door, it opened for them. Janine heard music. It was dark inside, so she couldn't see, but she stilled, almost afraid to move. Terri and Susan looped their arms with hers and dragged her inside.

Her first thought as she stepped into the expansive foyer was a mixture of then and now. Very old Hollywood mixed with the sound and sparkle of today. But not at all garish or disco-like. Instead, it was warm and welcoming. A rollicking beat of rhythm and blues pounded in her ears—sexy, making her pulse thrum with excitement.

But what really got her heart racing was the man walking their way. He wore a dark suit, white shirt halfway unbuttoned, revealing a light dusting of chest hair. He looked like he hadn't shaved today, but instead of looking unkempt, he looked...oh my God he looked sexy as hell. As he drew closer, she noticed he was staring right at her. In this sea of gorgeous women, his whiskey brown eyes were targeting her? And he was smiling. His lips were full and Janine's first thought was of what his mouth could do to a woman.

"*Bon soir, mademoiselles.* Welcome to Sneak Peek."

Holy crap. He had just the hint of a French accent, as if he'd lived in the States for years, but hadn't quite lost the inflection. Why were her panties getting wet? It wasn't like she didn't regularly meet handsome men in her line of work. Good-looking men walked every sidewalk in Los Angeles. You could run into them at the grocery store and down every aisle, since they were as plentiful as apples. But this one—damn—he hit her hot buttons in a major way.

"I'm Philippe Delacroix, but everyone calls me Del. In fact, if you call me Philippe or, God forbid, Phil, I won't answer you."

She smiled at that. He so didn't look like a Phil.

"I'm part owner of this club along with my friend, Alejandro Diaz, who I'm sure you'll see around here tonight. Please, come in and make yourselves comfortable."

Terri, Melinda and Susan said their hellos and rushed in, heading straight for the bar. In a damn hurry, she noted, all of them casting amused glances at Del and then back at her. She didn't quite know what happened, but it seemed as if they knew where they were going. One minute they were all standing there, the next the other three were gone. Janine found herself unable to move, her feet planted in the middle of the lobby like some mute, immobile dimwit. Del, at least, was polite enough to remain there with her so she didn't look like an imbecilic wall flower.

He cocked his head to the side. "Your friends left you."

"Seems that way."

"You look nervous as hell."

"That obvious, huh?"

"First time?"

She swallowed. "First time for what?"

"To visit the club."

She shook her head. "I don't even know where I am. My friends dragged me here and didn't tell me where we were going, so I'm sorry to say I have no clue what Sneak Peek is."

His lips curled in a hint of a smile. "Ah. Nice surprise."

She glared into the pitch black bar area, wondering where her so-called friends had disappeared to. "If you say so." Turning back to him, she realized he owned this club and she had probably just insulted him. "No offense. I'm sure this is a very nice place, but I'm not big on surprises."

"I can tell. Your body is as tense as a coiled-up snake. We need to relax you."

We? What is this we*?* "I'll be fine. I just need to find my friends."

"You need a drink. How about a tour?"

She definitely needed the drink. And the tour sounded nice. Anything to keep her away from the throng of bodies undulating in the overcrowded bar. Dancing was so not her thing, and knowing her friends, they'd drag her out there to bump and grind with a bunch of strange guys. Oh, God, there wasn't a male stripper review tonight, was there? She could so see Susan, Terri and Melinda thinking *that* was fun, especially tossing her to the wolves...er, naked dudes. Sweaty nude men giving her a birthday spanking. She'd die.

"Come on. You look like you're about to pass out."

Her gaze drifted up at Del, wondering what he saw when he looked down at her. Had she gone pale? Probably too much thought of Chippendale dancers and birthday spankings. She'd always had a way overactive imagination. He took her arm, and as she walked alongside him, she noted how warm his hand was, how easy he seemed to move, with such fluidity and grace. Like a sleek panther, comfortable in his skin.

She'd never once been comfortable in hers. She was jealous of people who were at ease in their environment. Del seemed relaxed, casting a genuine smile at people they passed by. He led her through a doorway and into a very casual room with a couple of beige chairs, a sofa and a huge mirror lining one wall. There was a bar off to one side, and the other side had tons of electronic equipment.

"Part of my office," he said, moving to the bar. "What would you like?"

"Rum if you have it. On the rocks would be fine."

He poured two glasses and handed her one. "I respect a woman who likes her liquor hard. Too many are into those fussy wines."

She snorted and accepted the glass from him. "Wine gives me a vicious headache the next day. Though I can suffer through it for business dinners." She was already regretting the champagne, knowing she'd feel the effects later. But it had served its purpose—it had taken the edge off her nervousness, at least for a little while.

He took a long swallow and nodded. "As we all must, on occasion."

My God, she couldn't get over how gorgeous he was. He smelled good, too, and not rife with cologne. She inhaled as he drew closer. More like soap. She almost laughed at that. He smelled freshly showered and clean, with an earthy undertone she could only describe as utter male scent. Primitive and oh so sexy.

Where had her mind gone, anyway?

"So you really have no idea what kind of place Sneak Peek is?" he asked, rimming his fingertip around the edge of the glass.

She followed his finger. Even that movement was sexy. God, she was pathetic. "No clue."

"I'm surprised your friends didn't warn you."

There went that half smile again, like he had a secret. A wicked one. *Uh-oh.* "Warn me?"

He took her glass and set it on the small table next to his, then drew his arm around her back and turned her toward the mirror. The mirror was long and tall as the wall in front of her. She looked at herself standing next to Del, at the way his hand casually rested against her hip, the way his thumb stroked over the fabric of her dress.

She felt what she saw reflected in the mirror—her skin burning up as the thin layer separating her body from his fingers didn't seem like nearly enough armor. She was going up in smoke, on fire from the way he looked at her, the way his eyes went dark, from a light whiskey to a deep brandy.

She started to turn away, but the slightest pressure of his hand held her in place. She realized, then, that she was alone in a room with a complete stranger. Her friends didn't know where she was. She didn't know where she was. Or who she was with.

"You're still tense."

"I'm...I'm sorry." She swept her hand over her hair. One strand had fallen loose, draping over her eye. She smoothed it back into place. "I think I should go find my friends."

"Your friends are fine. And so are you. Do I make you nervous?"

He wasn't tense at all, his body completely relaxed next to hers. "A little."

He moved away, giving her a couple inches of space. "I'm sorry. I can be a bit direct when I'm intrigued with a woman, and I'm used to...a different sort of female who frequents Sneak Peek. I didn't mean to make you uncomfortable."

Okay, now she really wanted to know where she was. "I'm not exactly uncomfortable. Just curious."

He lifted a brow. "How curious?"

"Tell me about your club." Forewarned was forearmed?

A knock at the door prevented his answer. "Come in," he said.

A gorgeous man entered, tall and tan and casting a gracious smile in her direction. Dressed similarly to Del, he moved into the room with the same casual grace. "Sorry, Del, I did not know you were occupied."

"It's all right. This is..." Del turned to Janine. "Damn. I don't even know your name."

"Janine," she said.

The man nodded. "Ah, the lovely Janine. Your friends were wondering where you had disappeared to." He walked over, swept her hand in his and pressed a light kiss to it. "I am Alejandro Diaz, one of the co-owners of the club."

"Oh, yes. Del mentioned you. Very nice to meet you. You said my friends were looking for me?"

"Yes."

"I should go then." She started toward the door, but Alejandro still held her hand. "Totally unnecessary. They were merely worried you had turned tail and left. I believe they said something to the effect of, 'chickening out'?"

That made her pause. "Chickened out? Hmph." She lifted her chin, insulted that her friends would think that of her, even if it was true. Though she still had no idea what she would be chickening out of. And she'd be damned if she'd let her friends goad her.

Del snorted. "You can tell them I'm giving Janine a tour and she's in good hands."

"I'll do that." Alejandro cast a knowing look in Del's direction. "You two have a wonderful evening."

Janine inclined her head. "It was very nice to meet you."

Alejandro shut the door behind him. Janine turned back to Del, who wore a very amused expression on his face.

"What?"

"Your friends thought you'd run."

She shrugged and took a long swallow of rum. It burned, but it felt good. Courage-inducing. "They're very adventurous. Me? Not so much."

"So, you're the conservative one in the group?"

"I'm hardly conservative." Boring, maybe, but not conservative. She led a wicked, sexy, adventurous lifestyle—in her fantasies. Her reality was something entirely different.

He drained his glass and set it back on the table. "Why do I get the feeling you're trying to convince me of something that's not quite true?"

"My friends, Susan, Terri and Melinda have fascinating lives. One's an author of mystery books who travels the world researching and doing nationwide book tours. One's an actress and the other's a model. Their careers alone are profoundly more exciting than mine."

"And what do you do?"

"I manage my father's estate. He's the late Louis Bartolino."

"Ah. I've heard of your father. My condolences on his death last year."

She nodded. "Thank you. I took over the Bartolino Foundation after his death. That's my work."

Del crossed his arms. "Big job for one person."

"It can be. I handle it. Nevertheless, it hardly makes me...exciting."

His lips twitched. "I don't know about that. I find you intriguing."

It would be rude to snort. "Right. Of course you do."

Del picked up their glasses and refilled their drinks. "Being exciting has nothing to do with your career, Janine. It's an inner quality, a glow." He walked back to her and handed her the glass, his fingers brushing hers. She felt a zing of electricity.

"You shine like a woman who has a secret."

"I have no secrets."

"Is that right. None at all?"

"No." She sipped the rum, wishing she'd never come in here. Del made her uncomfortable. He was too probing, as if he knew something about her that she didn't. Which was ridiculous.

"We all have secrets, Janine. Sometimes things even we aren't aware about ourselves."

"I'm an open book. Read the society section in the newspaper. You'll find out anything you want to know about me."

"That's surface. Public relations. That's not who you really are."

She shook her head, fighting back a laugh. "Really. You've known me for ten minutes. Who am I?"

He shrugged and moved away from her. "Not sure. Let's find out." He pressed a button next to the mirror and the lights went out.

Janine startled, not sure what was happening. But then the mirror glowed. No, wait. A picture was forming. What the hell was that?

It wasn't a picture. It was a two-way mirror. On the other side was a room, with a bed and a chair and nothing else.

There was a man and a woman in the room, both young and extremely attractive. The man was tall, well built, with cover model good looks. He was naked from the waist up, wore no shoes, only a pair of jeans with the top button undone. The woman had long blonde hair loosely cascading down her back. She wore only a scarlet red bra that barely contained her copious breasts, and a matching thong. She looked like she worked out, her body in fine shape. She was on her knees in front of the man, dragging the zipper down his jeans.

The blonde licked her lips, anticipation clearly showing on her face.

Janine licked her lips, too, her throat gone dry. What was she looking at? It was an intimate, personal moment between two people. She should turn away, walk out of the room, but she couldn't move. Her feet seemed to have glued themselves to the floor.

And her body's response to what she saw was off the charts. Her nipples tightened, her breasts felt hot and swollen, and her clit quivered. She was turned on in a major way, and she sent up a thankful prayer for the darkness surrounding her. What would Del think of her?

What kind of place was Sneak Peek?

As if in answer to her unspoken question, Del moved behind her, his body seemingly surrounding her, crowding her personal space. She inhaled, picking up his scent, letting it fill her. His cock was rigid against her ass as he pressed against her, letting his hands rest on her hips.

"Sneak Peek is a sex club, Janine. A club for voyeurs and exhibitionists. If you look across the room you'll see another window. There are over a dozen people watching."

She tore her gaze away from the couple, finding the window Del mentioned. Men and women stood on the other side of a glass enclosure, some fully clothed, others in various states of undress. Some merely observed, while there were some couples fondling each other as they watched.

"The couple you see in the other room are exhibitionists. They enjoy having sex knowing that others are watching. It heightens their pleasure. In this scenario, we're the voyeurs."

Oh, God. She shouldn't be here. Not this kind of place. For so many different reasons. Her head spun in a million directions, the urge to run strong.

But still, she couldn't tear her gaze away from the couple on the other side of the mirror, especially when the woman pulled the man's sizeable cock from his jeans and enveloped it between her full, painted lips. The look of ecstasy on the man's face made Janine's breath catch. The woman's gaze was glued to the man's as she sucked his cock in deep. With one free hand, the woman tucked her fingers into her own pussy and began to pleasure herself.

Janine's pussy quivered, as if she, too, could feel the sensation of finger fucking herself, could taste the man's thick cock between her lips, could feel the heated gazes of dozens of people watching them. She wanted to close her eyes and pretend she was anywhere but here.

At the same time, she couldn't deny that she wanted to *be* the woman on the other side of the mirror.

Chapter Two

Del never did the full court press on guests at the club, never insinuated his intentions, always let the women come to him. Frankly, a lot of women came to him. He didn't often have to search them out. He loved women, they knew it, and he could always find someone whose needs met his. That's what Sneak Peek was about—freedom to do whatever people wanted to do. If he and a woman found something in common, and there was mutual agreement, then a night of fun ensued. There were always signals, and he knew when a woman was coming on to him.

Janine hadn't come on to him at all. So what the hell was he doing pursuing her? She was uncomfortable as hell and he'd known it from the minute she'd stepped through the front door.

She'd also looked curious. When he'd spied the four ladies at the door, he'd done the host thing because his partner, Ali, had been otherwise engaged. They always liked to greet people whenever they could, make them feel comfortable and welcome, especially newcomers.

The four women walking in had been knockouts, but his gaze had landed on Janine, because she seemed to stand out. She wasn't even the most beautiful of the group, but there was something about her eyes...

She'd locked onto him right away, too, though he didn't know why. Not that it mattered. He'd read her signal as interest, and since her friends had so conveniently run off and left her with him, he'd grabbed her. And he hadn't yet been able to let go. Pretty damned unusual for him. Typically he'd make the rounds, and it wasn't until later in the evening, if at all, that he'd hook up with a woman.

Not tonight. He was a fairly good judge of a woman's interest. Janine might not have said it, but she was interested. Her green eyes spoke volumes, and what they said when he'd turned on the two-way mirror expressed more than mere interest. They screamed shock, but also curiosity, and then desire.

Like now. He couldn't see her eyes because he stood behind her, but he picked up the unmistakable scent of aroused female, inhaled it like the sweetest perfume. Her breathing came in short, shallow bursts, as if she was trying her damnedest to mask how much the scene in front of her turned her on.

It was a hot scene. Victoria and Jake were regulars, and really got into putting on a show. And Victoria could suck cock like she was born to it, taking Jake's shaft deep.

Del envied Jake at the moment, understood the almost pained look of utter rapture on Jake's face as Victoria deep throated him. Del's cock was hard, pressing against his pants. As close as he was to Janine, she had to be aware of that, a fact he didn't try to hide.

"You had no idea Sneak Peek was a sex club, did you?"

It took her a moment to answer, and when she did, her tone had dropped, her answer spilling out in a low, whispered breath that rumbled in his balls.

"No clue."

"Why did your friends bring you here?"

"I have no idea. A joke, I guess."

She wasn't laughing. She was barely breathing as she watched the couple through the window. Her entire body was tense, but was it nervousness or excitement? He pressed his fingers into her hips, staying close to her. She didn't pull away, a good sign. He liked the feel of her, the lush curve of her hips. She was built like a woman. She'd said her friends were the beautiful ones. He disagreed. They were all stick thin, and for the love of Christ, they all needed to eat a cheeseburger before they wasted away. He liked women with some flesh on them.

"They're doing this willingly?" she asked. "Having sex, knowing others are watching them."

"Yes. That's how they get off, the excitement of being watched."

He felt her shudder.

"This is unbelievable. I didn't even know places like this existed."

That's what he liked to hear. Sneak Peek was exclusive. He and Ali didn't have to advertise, their club was only for those who knew about it, recommended it to others who wanted a voyeuristic or exhibitionist adventure.

"I shouldn't be here," she said, finally dragging her gaze away from the couple.

"Why not?" Del didn't turn on the light.

"What if someone sees me here? Someone I know, who could leak it to the press. Do you know what that could do to my reputation?"

He laughed. "Your reputation is safe, as is the character of all our clients. Sneak Peek is discreet, has been since we opened. There are no cameras allowed here. No press is ever permitted inside or within the gates of our property. We have a very high class establishment, we cater to our clients and assure anonymity.

"You're safe here, Janine."

She wrapped her arms around her middle, half turning back to the window. "This isn't my kind of lifestyle. I don't...do this."

He smiled, though he knew she couldn't see his face in the darkened room. "You aren't required to *do* anything here other than enjoy yourself. That's likely why your friends brought you."

"I have no idea why they brought me here, what they were thinking. This is ridiculous. I need to go find them."

He moved to the wall and flipped on the switch, darkening the mirror and bringing up the lights in the room. "As you wish."

She blinked, then frowned. "I'm sorry. This has nothing to do with you. I mean no insult to you or to your club."

This time he knew she could see his face, and the corners of his lips lifted. "None taken. Come on. Let's locate your friends."

He led her out of the room and down the hall, back toward the lobby. "We'll start at the bar, since they headed that way when we first came in."

She stopped and turned to him. "You don't need to stay with me. I can find them by myself."

He arched a brow. "Are you trying to dump me?"

Her eyes went wide. "Oh, no. Not at all. But I'm certain you have other things you need to do."

"I was teasing you. And don't worry about me. I do whatever I want." And what he really wanted to do was Janine. She might act shocked and appalled, but her body's reaction had told another story. He wasn't finished with her yet. "I'd like to stay with you, make sure you're reunited safely with your friends. It's the least I can do. Besides, if they're not in the bar, you're not familiar with the club. You wouldn't know where to go to look for them. And I did promise you a tour."

She tilted her head. "All right. Thank you."

They entered the bar, which was actually a huge dance club. Music blared from the speakers, bodies were packed wall to wall. Del nodded to the bouncer as they entered through the open doorway. Business was booming, a very good thing.

Del laid his hand on the small of Janine's back, guiding her through the mob of people packed into the aisles. She looked for her friends, he followed along, trying to direct her through the walkways. Since he was taller, he had a better viewpoint for the seating areas.

"I don't see them," she said as they reached the other end of the bar.

"I didn't either." He searched the upper tiers where tables were situated, not seeing them there, either. "Come on." He took her hand and pulled her toward the dance floor.

She stood firm. "I...I don't dance."

"This is the best way to search for them on the dance floor. You can handle one dance, right?"

She sucked her bottom lip between her teeth. His cock responded with a resounding twitch.

"I suppose so."

"Come on. I'll try not to step on your toes." He grinned and led her onto the dance floor. As soon as they made their way into the middle of the throng, the music changed to something slow and sexy.

Perfect. He pulled Janine against him, wrapping one arm around her waist and gathering the fingers of one of her hands in his. Their gazes met. Hers was wide eyed and uncertain, and he found he liked her a little off-balance.

Their hips met, and Del led her in the slow, rhythmic beat.

She frowned. "You can dance."

He turned her, then tilted her in a half dip. She followed every move without stumbling. "So can you."

"I didn't say I couldn't. I just don't like to."

"Why not?"

She shrugged, but didn't answer. Instead, her gaze searched the dance floor, which gave him a chance to look at her, to enjoy feeling her body pressed up to his.

They fit well, her full breasts pillowed against his chest, her hips nestled inside his, making him wonder how her naked skin would feel sliding against his, her legs wrapped around him, his cock tucked inside her enveloping heat.

Not a good idea to be thinking about that. She'd made it clear she didn't belong here, that this wasn't her scene. Still, she was lying. To herself, maybe, as well as to him.

And Del loved a challenge. He didn't mind taking it one step at a time. Right now, she wasn't even stiff and unyielding in his arms, but letting him lead her in the dance, flowing in his arms, her body melding with his.

Why didn't she like to dance? She flowed into it, as if it were as natural to her as breathing.

Yeah, he liked the feel of her. He drew her closer, his lips brushing her earlobe.

"Do you see them?"

"No. I don't think they're in here anymore."

"Then I'll take you on that tour I promised, and we'll see if we can find them."

He lingered at her neck and inhaled, realizing she wore no perfume. He preferred a woman who relied on her natural scent instead of choking perfume or cologne. Janine smelled like her shampoo, and her own sweet skin. He resisted the urge to lick the pulse beating along the column of her throat, as tantalizing as that was.

She swallowed and tilted her head back to look up at him. "Shall we go, then?"

"Are you sure you can handle it, or would you rather wait here while I go search for your friends?"

Her lips pursed as if he'd insulted her. Good.

"I can handle it."

"You might see some things similar to what you saw in my office."

She lifted her chin. "I said I could handle it. I'm hardly a virgin."

He smiled. "Good to know."

"Are you baiting me, Del?"

"Probably. I can't help myself. I don't think you're as offended by what you saw as you'd like me to believe." He tucked her hand in the crook of his arm and led her off the dance floor, weaving them through the thick crowd and out the doorway.

"I never said I was offended," she said as soon as they cleared the noisy room. "I said it wasn't my cup of tea."

"Uh huh."

"Really. I'm sure whatever it is everyone does here is fine. It's just not for me."

"So you say."

She looked over at him. "You're very annoying."

"Not the first time I've heard that."

Despite her obvious irritation, the corners of her lips lifted.

"And you find it very hard to resist my incredible charm."

"I don't know about that. I find you all too resistible."

"We'll see." He moved through a doorway and into the private playrooms. People passed them in the halls, some half-dressed, hair mussed and a just-fucked smile on their faces. He nodded as they passed by, envying their satisfaction. His dick was twitching. Janine had affected him, and the smell of sex was strong here.

He opened a door and they entered a darkened room.

"What's this?" she asked, her voice lowering to a whisper.

"A scene. We can check for your friends here. They might have stopped in to watch."

He closed the door behind them, wondering how long it would take before Janine would want to bolt. This one was two men, one woman, and instead of a mirror to look through and watch, people crowded into the room with the threesome. Del led her to a spot against the wall, not more than ten feet from where the ménage was taking place.

Janine pressed her body back against his, as if by doing so she could get away from what she saw. But she didn't turn away or avert her gaze. Del stepped to her side and she backed against the wall.

He wanted to look at her face.

Her eyes were wide, but her expression wasn't one of disgust or horror.

The woman on display kneeled on the bed, her mouth engulfing a thick cock, her legs spread and taking another dick in her pussy. Just as Del suspected, Janine was entranced by what she saw. She swallowed, her mouth open, her pink tongue flicking out to lick over her bottom lip. He watched her breasts rise and fall with her rapid breaths, her hands clench at her sides, then rub against her dress. She shifted on one foot, then the other, as if she couldn't quite stand still.

Around them were the sounds of heavy breathing. Some of the guests touched themselves, or rubbed against their partner's genitals.

Foreplay. And Janine had to hear and see what was going on around her. She wasn't unaffected.

He knew all the signs. Despite her insistence that voyeurism wasn't her thing, he could tell she was turned on. He'd bet his ownership in Sneak Peek that her nipples were tight and her pussy was wet. If he slid his hand up under her dress and started rubbing her clit, would she let him? Would she turn from voyeur to exhibitionist? His cock hardened at the thought.

The moaning and sucking sounds grew louder as the frenzy intensified. The woman took the cock deep in her mouth, wrapping both hands around the thick shaft. When she withdrew, she stroked it and licked the wide purple head, then swirled her tongue over it, capturing the white pearly liquid escaping the tip. The man at her head grasped the back of the woman's neck and directed her mouth back over his cock, while the man behind her gave her a hard fucking, spreading her ass cheeks apart so he could show the woman's pussy and his dick sliding into it.

Janine was focused on the threesome, not searching for her friends. She hadn't once surveyed the other people gathered in the room watching the scene.

"Do you see your friends in here?" he asked.

It took her a few seconds to tear her gaze away from the ménage. "What? Oh." Only then did she look around the room, scanning the two dozen or so people. "No. They're not here."

"Would you like to stay and watch the scene play out?"

She shook her head, but she was watching the threesome the entire time. He led her out the door, but he sensed her reluctance. Too bad, because it looked like a triple orgasm was imminent. That was a great scene.

"So, they weren't in there. Next room," he said.

"There's more?" She blew out a breath.

He tried not to laugh. "If you'd like, I can just check the rooms and you can wait outside. I did meet your friends so I know what they look like."

"No, that's okay. You only saw them for a few seconds. You might not notice them in a crowded room. I'd better go in with you."

"Janine! There you are."

He and Janine both turned. The woman walking down the hall was one that had come in with Janine tonight.

"Susan. Where the hell did you all disappear to?" Janine hurried to her friend.

Susan's face flushed with color. "We've been here and there. We've just been popping in and out of rooms, checking out the action." Susan looked around Janine at Del. "I see you've been doing the same thing with your friend here. Isn't this place great?"

"Oh yeah," Janine said, half turning to cast a sideways glance at Del. "Just great."

"Come on, Janine. You have to admit this is one hell of a party. Sneak Peek is wild!"

"Wild. Yes. Definitely."

Susan rolled her eyes. "I can tell you aren't yet into the spirit of fun." She looked at Del. "Has she gone hot and crazy and started ripping her clothes off yet?"

Del rubbed his nose. "Uh, not exactly."

"Danced on a tabletop?"

He snorted. "Not yet, but I'd pay money to see it."

Susan laughed. "I like you. You'd be a good influence on her."

"Susan, really," Janine said. "Where are your other two partners in slime?"

"Orgy room. It's amazing in there. Talk about eye candy." She held out her hand. "Come on, I'll take you there."

"I don't think so. I...have this god-awful headache. From the champagne, I think."

Susan frowned. "Oh, honey. I'm so sorry."

"Yeah, I think I'm going to call it a night. Say my goodbyes to the girls. I'll catch a cab home."

"Are you sure?"

She nodded. "Definitely. You go have fun."

Susan grinned. "I intend to." She hugged Janine. "Love you, honey. Happy birthday."

After Susan walked away, Del said. "It's your birthday?"

"Yes. My thirtieth."

"Happy birthday."

"Thank you."

"Sorry about your headache."

"I'll be all right. I had champagne earlier and it always gives me a headache. I should have known better."

He directed her down the hall. "I'll have a cab brought to the club for you."

"Thank you."

She didn't have a headache and he knew it. She'd loved what she'd seen of the club so far, so why did she balk at her friend's invitation to see more of it? What was she afraid of?

He took her back into his office. "Have a seat." He picked up the phone. "Mike, bring the car around front. I'd like you to drive a VIP guest home. Give me a call when it's ready."

After he hung up, Janine said, "You could just call a taxi for me."

"It's the least I can do for the birthday girl."

Her face tinged with pink and she looked down at her hands clasped in her lap.

Del sat on the corner of his desk, studying her. She was such a contrast. A sensual beauty, yet a lot of reticence about her, as if there was something she wanted but was afraid to ask for it.

"Janine."

She looked up. "Yes?"

"What is it about enjoying your own pleasure that scares you so much?"

Her brows knit together. "I don't understand your question."

"I could tell you were aroused by what you saw tonight, yet you keep denying that Sneak Peek has any appeal for you."

"I think you're presuming too much. You know nothing about me or how I feel about this place."

Ignoring her comment, he said, "We all have a dark side, you know."

"I don't."

"I think you're lying. The big question is, are you lying just to me, or to yourself, too."

"That's almost insulting."

He smirked. "Almost, but not quite? Because there's a tinge of truth in what I said?"

She stood and smoothed her dress. "I'll just wait out front."

She started for the door, but before she got there, Del said, "I'll bet you masturbate all the time."

She paused, turned to him. "What?"

"In your fantasies, you envision yourself being watched as you touch yourself. You also like to watch others having sex. It turns you on so much, makes you so wet, it gets you off like a rocket. I'll bet you're a screamer when you come, hoping someone will hear you. You want people to see you with your legs spread, your fingers fucking your pussy, rubbing your clit, tweaking your nipples."

She didn't answer, but her face and neck were bright pink. And she was still immobile, hadn't walked out of the room.

He smiled. "No, I don't have hidden cameras in your bedroom. I just know you."

"How?"

He'd barely heard the word, she'd whispered it with such a soft voice.

"I know what you need."

She shook her head. "No, you don't. You don't know me at all. I live a life above reproach. I'm in the public eye. I could never do...this. My family's reputation is everything to me. My father's legacy is what I work to maintain."

"Your father's legacy would be safe if you went out and had a little fun, explored what you like."

"No. I can't."

His phone rang, signaling the car was ready. He took a card from his pocket and walked over to her, slipping it in her hand. "Call me if you change your mind and want to explore that dark side. Stop looking over your shoulder, afraid of your own shadow. There's a life you're missing out on."

She turned and left the room without saying a word to him.

Del sat behind his desk and dragged his fingers through his hair.

Smooth move, Delacroix. And you call yourself a ladies man. The most intriguing woman he'd met in years and he'd just insulted her, then let her walk out of his life.

Maybe he was losing his touch.

Janine closed her front door, kicked off her shoes and walked straight into her bedroom, tossing her things onto her dresser.

"Dark side. As if he knows anything at all about me." She stalked into the dressing area and shrugged out of her dress, hung it up, then did her before bed routine, brushing her teeth, washing her face and taking down her hair. After ruthlessly combing out the hairspray, she felt better. A little bit, anyway. She walked into the bedroom and passed by the dresser, noticing the card Del had given her.

Call me if you change your mind and want to explore that dark side.

She was still irritated by Del's words. What did he know of her life? How dare he presume to make judgments about her?

Naked, she slid under the covers and pushed the button on the television remote, then turned off her bedside lamp. There was a DVD already in the player and she pressed the play button. The screen brought up a scene very similar to the one that occurred in the last room she and Del had been in tonight. People standing around watching a woman getting fucked by two men. It was one of her favorites.

And no doubt why Del's words had made her so uncomfortable.

It was if he'd seen right through her—as if he knew her, everything about her—about her fantasies. As if he knew her weaknesses.

No. not weaknesses. Choices. She'd chosen the life she lived, she wasn't imprisoned by it. How ridiculous to think otherwise.

The couple on the screen mimicked what she'd seen live tonight. God, that had been exciting, standing in the same room where a threesome was occurring, being able to watch it live instead of on a television screen. She'd had to resist raising her dress and touching herself right there. Because if someone in the room had recognized her, caught her masturbating in public...

Despite the horror a reality like that would bring, the fantasy was something entirely different. She would have loved nothing more than to lean against the wall tonight, spread her legs and lift her dress, let Del see her black thong panties. They were so wet...soaked, actually. Could he smell the aroused scent of her pussy? He'd stayed close to her the entire time. She knew he was attracted to her. It was a heady experience, having a man like Del's interest. Not at all typical of the type of guy she usually dated. She usually went for the buttoned up businessman, not the laid back, kind of rough looking type. Yet she couldn't help but imagine what his beard stubble would feel like against her thighs while he was between her legs licking her pussy.

A rush of heat made her nipples tingle. What she needed was a good orgasm to relieve the stress, then sleep. Tomorrow she'd forget all about tonight's disaster.

She tugged her bottom lip between her teeth and kicked the covers off, pushing them to the end of the bed. Planting her feet flat on the mattress, she guided her fingers between her legs. She focused on the television, on the woman who was the center of attention in a crowd of people.

"Yes, watch me," she whispered, becoming the woman in the video, then the woman she'd seen in the room at Sneak Peek tonight, anywhere where she could be seen. "Look at my pussy, watch me touch myself."

Sensation rolled and centered between her legs, every nerve ending bundled with tension. What would it be like to be that focus of attention, to know others watched her have sex?

Despite her determination to forget all about Del, her fantasies went haywire and she was propelled back to Sneak Peak, into that room where others stood against the wall. Only this time, she was the naked woman in the center of the room, and the man with her was Del.

She sighed, closed her eyes and let her fingers drift over her pussy, circling her clit. Only her hands became Del's hands, larger, rougher with a more determined stroke over her soft flesh. He would take charge, know what she liked, where she needed to be touched.

"Here?"

She heard his voice against her ear, his warm breath at her neck. She shivered as he swept his hand over her clit. "Yes, right there."

When he paused, his hand pressing down on that tight bundle of nerves, her hips shot off the bed, wanting more of that exquisite pleasure.

Oh, this wasn't going to take long. She was too primed, too ready for the explosion. But she wanted it to last, loved his touch. It had been too long since a man had touched her, had petted her naked skin. And it had never happened in front of an audience like this.

She took a moment to glance over at the crowd—shadows mostly—all she could see in the darkened recesses of the room, but she knew they were there, watching her, watching the two of them. She spread her legs wider, wanting them to see everything, to know what she was feeling.

Del climbed onto the bed behind her and held her up so she could watch them. Now she was the voyeur, because the people around her were touching themselves, touching each other, turned on by watching her. It only added to her frenzy.

"Yes, come with me. Make me come." It was dual pleasure, the ultimate fantasy. They were all going to make each other come. Del moved to her side and she reached for his cock, wrapping her fingers around the heated steel of his flesh. She began to stroke it up and down in rhythm to the others masturbating. Surges of pleasure flowed within her, concentrating directly on her clit and pussy.

She wanted to be fucked. She wanted Del to really be here, sinking his cock deep in her, so her pussy would grip it tight when she came. She wanted him to fuck her until she couldn't breathe anymore.

But that wasn't reality. She was in a fantasy, a delicious fantasy that was taking her to the height of pleasure, and she couldn't hold back any longer.

"Faster." She looked down at Del's hand, at the way he moved it in soft circles over her clit, then dipped down in the cleft of her pussy and finger fucked her. He ground his palm against the hard knot and she splintered, pulsing against his fingers, pouring her juices over him. Wave after wave crashed over her as she gripped his cock, watched him come all over her belly and hip, her gaze flitting from Del to the others in the room.

It was a heady, amazing experience, and over all too soon, leaving her shattered, spent, and once again alone in the reality of her bedroom.

Exhausted, she turned off the movie and television and lay in the darkness, pulling the covers up over her.

The orgasm should have relieved her stress, cleared her mind so she could sleep. Instead, she felt more pent up, her thoughts refusing to scatter.

As she closed her eyes, the image of Del was still imprinted firmly in her mind.

She couldn't. She wouldn't dare.

It wasn't going to happen.

Chapter Three

Two days. It had been two days and she still couldn't get Del out of her mind. Or that damn club, either.

His card still sat on her dresser, and every morning and every night when she walked by it, she was reminded of her experience there.

She had to push it all out of her thoughts. A place like that wasn't for her. He wasn't for her. She was too often in the public eye, always written up and photographed for the newspaper's society page. What would happen if she was discovered to be frequenting a voyeurism and exhibitionism club? The scandal would ruin the foundation. Her father would roll over in his grave. The Bartolino name would be shamed.

Sometimes it didn't matter what her needs and desires were. She had to think of the family name first. Her father had always taught her that the foundation came first, that name was everything. When he knew he was sick and wasn't going to recover, he told her over and over again that reporters were vicious, that they would use anything they could against her. That she should find a nice, rich, stable man with no skeletons in his closet and get married, raise a family and carry on the foundation's work.

Her father had mapped out her future for her. She was all that was left of the Bartolinos. She'd never let him down by besmirching the family name.

And yet, Del continued to creep into her thoughts. Wicked sexy, gorgeous, seemingly so carefree. She envied him.

But dammit, how could Del seem to know so much about her, how could he have spent so little time with her, yet have such an intimate knowledge of her sexual desires?

I know what you need.

His words haunted her.

She shuddered, then cast the thoughts aside. Tonight was not a night to be thinking about Del. Or about sex. Not at a black tie dinner, dance and silent auction for the Bartolino Foundation's favorite children's hospital charity. She was "on" tonight and in charge, and there were five hundred guests who'd paid two thousand dollars a plate about to enter the ballroom at one of the most prestigious Beverly Hills hotels. She was determined to make this the most successful year ever.

The doors opened, the crowds spilled in, and Janine engaged herself in playing hostess. She knew almost everyone in attendance, people who were prominent in the community, the top of the social ladder in either business, politics or the entertainment field. She felt at ease with all of them, having done this since she was a child and accompanying her parents to events like this.

She had been trained well. Even after her mother passed away when Janine was twelve, she had started acting as hostess at her father's side. He had always told her how much he depended on her, how one day she would take over the foundation and run it.

Jaci Burton

And now, she was. She'd never considered it a burden, though she'd often wished for brothers and sisters so she wouldn't be so lonely.

On a night like this she missed her father. Now she had no family left, and for the first time since his passing she really felt that sense of being utterly alone in the world. Good thing she had competent staff at the foundation to assist her.

She sighed, then turned and smiled at one of the chief benefactors of the foundation. Stefan Montrose, in his fifties, divorced three times, a notorious womanizer, tabloid fodder, and constantly trying to get her into his bed.

He lifted her hand and pressed a kiss to her knuckles.

"You look amazing tonight, Janine."

"Thank you, Stefan. So do you. And where is your lady du jour?"

He shrugged. "Powdering her nose or whatever it is the women do en masse when four or five of them run off together. And where is your date for the evening?"

"I don't have one. I'm much too busy to entertain someone."

"Ah. Too bad. If I'd known, I'd have been more than happy to act as your escort."

Oh, right. Like she didn't have enough to worry about without having to constantly fight off Stefan's hands wandering down the front of her dress, and hoping a reporter wouldn't get a picture of it. "That's very nice of you, Stefan, but I'm sure your little black book is already overflowing. I'm not interested in being added to the list."

He laughed. "I'd give it all up for you, Janine."

"And I'll bet you really do say that to all the girls."

"You know me all too well. How sad."

Despite her knowledge of Stefan's motives, she couldn't help but like him. He might be transparent, but he was honest about his intentions. "You'll have to work harder to be mysterious."

"I'll try, but I think your father ruined all chances I had with you by spilling all my sordid secrets."

She nodded. "I'm afraid so. He left no stone unturned. Really, Stefan, I'm amazed you don't make the front of *The Enquirer* every week."

"It's a goal of mine, didn't I tell you? I want to be scandal monger of the year."

She couldn't hold the snort inside. "If anyone can do it, you can."

"Thanks, Janine. I think I'll go find my date now. At least she still has illusions about me."

"Your secret is safe with me."

Stefan kissed her cheek and moved off into the crowd.

"One of your many admirers?"

Janine whirled at the voice behind her. Her smile died as recognition dawned.

"Del? What are you doing here?"

His lips curled. "I was invited."

She frowned. "You were? By whom?"

He shrugged. "By whomever does those things for your foundation, I imagine."

Just looking at him made her mouth water. Dressed casually at the club, he was delectable and sexy. In black tux, he was devastating. This was a man who could be comfortable dressed to the nines or lazing about in jeans. And he still sported that scruffy unshaven look, even in his tux. God, he was handsome. His dark eyes that seemed to be able to see through her just made her melt.

Then recognition dawned as she remembered his introduction the other night. "Delacroix Motors. Foreign imports."

He nodded. "Yes."

That's why he was on the guest list. Very important businessman. Lucrative company, too. The foundation had worked with his company before, and Delacroix had always been extremely generous. She didn't know why she hadn't made the connection the other night. Probably because she didn't expect the head of Delacroix Motors to have anything to do with owning and operating a sex club.

"What?" Del asked.

"I'm just...stunned."

"Why?"

"Because you're a prominent member of the community. And you own a..."

"Club for voyeurs and exhibitionists?"

"Shhh." She dragged him over to a corner of the room, out of earshot of the other guests. "I can't believe you're so blasé about this."

His lips curled. "That's because I don't give a shit what people think. You should try it sometime."

"Easy for you to say. If anyone found out I was there the other night—"

"What? The world would stop turning? The stars would fall from the sky? The global markets would all crash?"

She sniffed. "That's not funny."

"Nothing would happen, Janine. You're entitled to a life."

"Not that kind of a life."

"Why not?"

"Because the newspapers would drool over news like that. They'd love nothing more than to dig up some dirt about me, to muddy the pristine reputation of the foundation."

Del shook his head. "You're way too paranoid."

"Not at all. I've seen it happen. When you're in the limelight, the paparazzi stalk you just waiting for you to slip."

He turned around. "Nobody's even looking in our direction, not the slightest bit interested in you and I talking."

"That's because they wouldn't expect anything to happen here."

Del arched a brow. "Kind of gives one ideas, doesn't it?"

Despite her irritation, she flushed with heat. "It doesn't give me any ideas."

"That's okay. I have plenty for both of us. Come on. Let's dance."

"I told you I don't...Del!"

Too late. He'd grabbed her hand and tugged her through the crowd and toward the dance floor. Short of causing a scene by digging in her heels and wrenching away from his grip, she was stuck having to go along with him. Dammit.

The dance floor was crowded, as well it should be. She'd hired a fabulous orchestra, the strains of violins playing a slow, seductive melody. Del pulled her to the middle of the floor and drew her against him.

"You look beautiful in gold," he said, once again showing his prowess as a dancer, gliding her with no effort through the dance. "You dress to show off your body."

She looked down at the dress, glittering, floor-length and hugging her curves. She loved this dress because it sparkled.

She loved the slit in the middle because it showed off a little leg, her best feature, and hoped it would detract attention away from the fullness of her hips. Did she buy it to exhibit her body? Hardly. She'd never thought about that. This event was for the foundation, not to catch a man.

"I do not."

"There's nothing wrong with showing off your assets. You have a beautiful body."

"You're full of shit."

"And you need to work on your self esteem. Maybe you need to spend more time looking in the mirror. Naked."

"I don't have body image issues. Nor do I spend my time staring at myself naked in the mirror."

"Try it sometime," he said, his gaze roaming toward her breasts. "You might enjoy it."

She shook her head. "You and I are from completely different worlds, Del."

"I don't think so. I live in the same world you do. I run a successful business, am publicly involved in the community, but no one knows what I do for fun. I'm very discreet, but I enjoy my pleasures. I've spent several years as the owner of Sneak Peek while still maintaining Delacroix Motors, and guess what? No one has ever found out, because it's none of their business and I make sure to keep it that way."

"Lucky for you that you have that anonymity."

"And I think you want what I have to offer. You're just afraid to take that step."

"I'm not afraid. I'm just not interested."

The smile he cast wasn't smug, exactly...more triumphant. "You're worried. You think people watch you all the time. Look around. No one is paying attention to us."

She did. As Del turned her, she gazed at the others on the dance floor. None of them looked at her. They were focused on their partners. And beyond the dance floor, people were talking amongst themselves or busying themselves at the back tables where the silent auction was going on.

Still, she felt eyes on her. Why? Why couldn't she let go, as Del suggested?

"I could touch you intimately right here on the dance floor and no one would notice."

Her breath caught and she shook her head, her traitorous body responding to his suggestion with a quiver of anticipation. "No."

"The lights are low over the dance floor, the crowd noisy. People are packed in and enjoying each other. If I moved my hand like this..." His hand at her back traveled down, over her buttocks, gently caressing her. Janine sucked in her bottom lip as he palmed her ass and pulled her tighter into his embrace.

"It's just a dance, Janine. Relax and enjoy it."

He moved her through the steps, but her mind was lost as his hand grazed the curve of her hip, then across the front, dipping down to the slit in her dress. Okay, so it was dark on the dance floor but—

Oh, God. His hand made contact with her skin, his fingers creeping along her bare thigh. Part of her wanted to push him back, to walk away. But the other part of her, the part that kept her on the dance floor, was excited. Her pussy moistened, her nipples beading against the fabric of her dress. He wasn't stopping there either. As he drew her closer, he brushed her panties with the tips of his fingers.

"Del, stop." Whose breathless voice was that? Surely not hers.

"Do you really want me to stop?" He was so close his breath tickled her ear. "No one can see us, *ma beauté*. It's just you, and me. Doesn't it excite you knowing that I can touch you like this in a room full of people? That no one will know?"

He didn't wait for her answer, not that she could speak, anyway. Her protest had been weak at best, and now she had no voice at all. Her gaze was on him and him alone, her body concentrating on his touch as he rimmed the hem of her panties—so, so close to her pussy. She trembled in his arms as he rocked them back and forth to the music. They weren't even moving anymore. Did people notice?

Did she care?

Not anymore. Not when the tip of his finger traced upward, sliding along her clit. She sucked in a little gasp, and was met with a wicked smile in return.

"You're wet."

She nodded.

"I wonder how fast I could make you come, Janine?"

Pretty damn fast considering what that single touch had done to her. He shifted, making motions as if they were still dancing. His fingers danced too, up and down her swollen, trembling cleft, pressing along her agitated clit. She widened her stance, giving him access, wishing she hadn't worn panties so she could feel his fingers on her flesh. Gone was the reticence, the shock, the wondering what others would think. Del had her mesmerized and fully under his control with the magic of his touch. Thankfully, he did look around the room. Maybe he was checking to make sure they were safe and secure, that prying eyes didn't catch on to what he was doing. She could care less. She was single-minded in purpose now, and that was only to continue the amazing sensations of his fingers dipping into her crevice, promising delicious rewards.

She wanted that reward, clenched her fingers into the fabric of his tux jacket. He leaned against her and she felt the hard ridge of his cock against her hip. Oh how she wanted to rest her palm there, to stroke along his ridged length. She swallowed, wishing she could wrap her legs around his waist and feel him plunge inside her. She was so wet now, trembling with sensation overload, with the reality of this fantasy come to life.

"Yes," he said, moving his fingers in a torturous circle around the nub, then leaned forward to whisper in her ear again. "Come for me. Right here."

Oh, God. She really was going to. Right here, in public. Her fantasy was about to come true. The tight coil of sensation built and she couldn't hold back.

Look at me, people. I'm coming. Her body burst in climax and she shook in his arms. She fought for silence, clamping her lips together to fight back a moan. Del tightened his hold around her, palmed her pussy, dipping inside her panties to slide along her wet slit as she shuddered through the wild orgasm that threatened to drop her to the ground. If not for Del holding her, she wasn't sure what she would have done.

Panting, struggling to look normal, she closed her legs and Del withdrew his hand, then brought his fingers to his mouth and tasted her.

"So sweet. Just as I imagined you'd be. It's a damn good thing I have a tux jacket to hide my hard-on. Goddamn, Janine."

He sucked in a breath and twirled her around the floor as if nothing had just happened. Inside, she was still quaking from the aftereffects of one tremendous orgasm.

Nothing? Dear God, what had she done? She'd completely lost her mind. A mind that was still half in a sensual haze of pleasure.

Horrified, she glanced around the dance floor, but the couples weren't even looking their way.

"No one knows. Just you and me," he said, his gaze dark.

"I can't believe I did that."

He led her off the dance floor and to the table where drinks were served, grabbing two glasses of champagne and offering one to her. She took it and forced herself not to gulp it down. Her throat was dry as a desert from panting her way through her orgasm.

"Are you sure that champagne won't give you a headache?" he teased, obviously remembering her excuse from the other night at the club.

"I'll chance it." The champagne tasted fabulous, cool and refreshing, clearing her head. How could she do that? She was in charge of this entire event, and she'd just had almost-sex on a crowded dance floor. What if someone had gone looking for her? Good God she was losing her grip on reality.

"Now you're second-guessing yourself," he said, his wry grin annoying as hell.

"Quit reading my mind. It pisses me off."

He laughed. "You think too much. You need to turn your mind off and just let yourself enjoy."

"I can't. I have too many responsibilities."

"I'll tell you what. Go play nice hostess. But when the event is over, meet me outside."

"Why?"

"Because we're going to play tonight."

He didn't ask. Did she need him to? Despite the orgasm he'd given her on the dance floor, she wanted more. She wanted *him*. Inside her. She wanted to know where this was going to go. But here and now? No, she couldn't do that.

But doing anything with Del was risky. Anything public, anyway. She could, of course, date him, do things normal couples would do. But somehow she didn't think that's what he had in mind. He asked things of her that were impossible to give. Then again, maybe she was off-base about his intent. Maybe that's all he wanted, was to spend time with her in the way that couples normally spent time with each other. Dinner, movies and the like.

Right. And there really was a tooth fairy. She knew that's not what he wanted from her, and she had good reason for her trepidation.

But when was the last time you felt this alive? When was the last time your body throbbed like this?

"All right." The words spilled from her lips before she had the chance to take them back.

He nodded. "I'll be out front waiting when the event is over. Black Navigator." He turned and walked away, disappearing into the crowd.

Janine finally exhaled, then wondered what she'd just agreed to.

Chapter Four

Four hours later and Del's cock was still hard. Jesus, it wasn't like this was his first experience with a woman, or that he'd never had risky encounters before.

What was it about Janine that made her so different from other women, that made being with her such a turn on? Maybe because the other women had been so willing and eager, experienced at this game, and Janine was so hesitant? Maybe that was it, the lure, the challenge.

He hadn't been challenged in far too long. Not that he was bored. Hell, he loved the game and never tired of it. But with Janine...there was just something about her. Something fresh and innocent—almost...untouched about her. Because she was new at this. She hadn't done it. But she really wanted to.

In a way, that made her a virgin. And damn if that didn't turn him on.

You're such a fucking pervert, Delacroix.

He'd waited through the endless hours of dinner, small talk and the auction, until the ballroom was almost empty, knowing Janine wouldn't leave until the last of her guests was gone. When he was certain she was almost finished, he left, had his car brought around, then pulled up to the front of the hotel and parked there, waiting.

Would she show, or would she change her mind?

After almost thirty minutes, he was about to give up, but then a flash of gold at the revolving doors caught his eye. A swish of flowing gown, and there she was, strolling through the doors like Cinderella leaving the ball.

One look at her and his pulse started to race. She really did wear the look of a princess well, from her hair piled on top of her head, to the way the gown flowed around her legs. She wore a wrap covering her bare shoulders, but that only added to the allure. She glowed from head to foot, and he wanted to see more of her skin.

She spotted his car, stalled for a fraction of a second, then, when he stepped out and moved to the passenger's side to open her door, started walking toward him.

"I wasn't sure you'd come," he said.

"I wasn't sure I would, either."

"Don't be afraid, princess. I won't bite." As he held her hand and helped her slide into the front seat, he added, "Unless you ask me to."

She slanted a wary glance at him and he closed the door, moving around to the driver's side.

"Where are we going?" she asked as he put the car into gear.

He moved onto the boulevard. "For a drive." He pressed the button and opened the moon roof. "It's a beautiful night. You can actually see the stars."

She tilted her head back, allowing him to ogle the soft column of her throat. "So you can. But that still doesn't tell me where we're going."

"It's a surprise. Trust me."

She was silent then while they drove out of the city and climbed into the hills. He knew exactly where he wanted to take her. The perfect spot for what he had in mind.

"How did the fundraiser go?" he asked, hoping to put her at ease with banal conversation.

"Great. We raised more money than last year, and that's always the goal."

"You do a wonderful job with the foundation. Your father would be proud."

"It was his life's work. I can only hope to do half as well as he did."

He got the idea Janine was worried she couldn't measure up. She needn't be. The foundation was a well oiled machine. It practically ran itself and was operated by competent staff. "You need to relax."

She stared ahead, but her lips curled in a half smile. "Probably."

"Have more fun."

"So my friends keep telling me."

"You should listen to them."

"Look where that brought me."

"To Sneak Peek?"

"Yes."

"And that's a bad thing?"

"The jury's still out on that one."

He pulled up the long drive, then stopped at the end of the bluff. "I'll have to hope for an innocent verdict, then."

She looked turned to him. "Where are we?"

"Lover's Lane."

Rolling her eyes, she said, "Seriously."

"A private overlook. Now quit asking questions and look."

He loved this view, and hoped it caught her the same way it had him. She finally turned away from him and looked through the windshield. Then her eyes widened.

"Oh, my. It's lovely."

They could see all of the city below them. It was clear, she could see the bright lights for miles. And above them, the stars were lit like brilliant sparklers over a stark black backdrop.

Janine undid her seatbelt, kicked off her shoes and stood in the seat, climbing through the moon roof to gaze at the stars.

"It's gorgeous, Del."

He grinned. He'd been right bringing her here, knowing she'd appreciate getting away from the cluttered city. Not every woman could understand the beauty, but somehow he'd known Janine would. He popped open his door and climbed out on the side so he could see her, planting his arms on the roof. "Thought you might enjoy it."

"It's stunning."

Silhouetted against the night sky, her hair shone as if the stars had fallen on it, darkness with golden brilliance. He wanted to remove every pin from her hair and see what it looked like tumbled against her face. Impulse won out, and he reached across the vehicle, pulling one loose strand across her cheek.

Janine followed the movement with her eyes, and her nonverbal response told him everything he needed to know. He climbed down, popped open the back of the Lincoln, then walked around to the passenger side, opened the door and swept her into his arms.

She didn't speak this time, didn't protest or ask what he was doing.

He'd already taken out the third row of seats so there was plenty of room. He sat her in the back on the plush carpet, then pushed the back seats forward, making even more room for them, climbing in and tugging her forward.

Now he had all the time in the world. He reached for the back of her hair and started pulling pins. Janine watched him in silence as he drew her hair forward, combing it with his fingers until it fell in soft sable waves around her shoulders.

A golden goddess. Seductive and innocent. One powerful punch to his senses. "You take my breath away."

"I'll bet you say that to all the girls," she said, her lashes sweeping down to caress her cheeks.

He tipped her chin up with his fingers, forcing her gaze to meet his. "I've never said that to any woman before." And that was true. He leaned in and swept his lips against hers. She tasted like strawberries and champagne, sweet and tart, just like the woman. He slid his tongue between her parted lips and licked along the velvet softness of her mouth. When she moaned in response, he gathered her into his arms and dragged her against him, plunging his fingers into the wild softness of her hair.

There was nothing tentative about her response to his kiss. She wrapped her tongue around his, licking as if she were dying for a taste of him. His cock hardened and pressed against his pants, his thoughts running wild. Her tongue was soft, wet, hot, and he could already imagine her licking his cock head and taking his shaft in her mouth, could already envision her on her knees while he wrapped her silken tendrils around his hand and helped guide her movements.

She pressed her palms against his chest and for a moment he thought she was going to push him away. But she slid them upward, trying to remove his jacket. He broke the kiss, shrugging out of the jacket and removing his tie. Her eyes were glittering with desire, reflecting the same brilliance of the stars, completely mesmerizing him with her siren's beauty.

He reached behind her to pull her against him again, this time locating the zipper on her dress. When he started to tug, she stilled, drew back, her eyes widening.

"Out here?"

"Yes."

She looked around. The tailgate was open, they were outside, and he knew her question.

"Yes, Janine. Out here. I want you naked under the stars."

Her lips were parted, her breathing quick and hard. She nodded, and he resumed unzipping her dress, then peeled it down to her waist, baring her breasts. Perfect, with ripe, dark nipples that were already peaked and begging for his lips to surround them.

She tilted her head and arched her back, an unconscious movement, but an invitation nonetheless. He leaned forward and grasped one breast in his hand, then licked around the dark nipple before capturing the bud between his lips and sucking on it.

Janine gasped, then cupped the back of his neck and held on as he licked her, toying with her nipple until it was hard and glistening with his saliva. He moved to the other breast, loving the feel of her pliant flesh in his hand, the way she was so responsive to his touch, his mouth, letting him know with her soft whimpers and her movements that she liked what he did to her.

"Del." His name was a soft whisper on her lips, and it made his balls quiver.

"Yeah, babe. I know." He pushed her back so she was lying down, then dragged the heavy dress off, leaving her clad in only her panties. The sexy little thing that barely covered her mound, the one he'd rubbed against on the dance floor. He draped her dress over the back of the front seat, then parted her legs, sweeping his hands down her thighs. She trembled.

"Shhh, relax."

"I...can't."

"Sure you can." He crawled between her legs, kissed her knees on the way down, then her inner thighs, finally settling on that spot that he'd wanted to be near all night long. She smelled musky, sweet, hot and turned on, and he recalled the taste of her on his fingers after she'd climaxed on the dance floor. He'd damn near come in his pants doing it to her, feeling her shudder and quake in his arms. She'd given him everything.

He wanted more. He buried his face against her panties and blew a warm breath against the silk.

"Oh, God, Del. Please."

He liked listening to her voice. He liked the sounds she made, even just hearing her breathe. All of it told him what she was feeling. He wanted her relaxed—he wanted her to come again.

He reached for the tiny strings at her hips and drew them down her thighs, keeping his gaze focused on her face as he pulled them over her legs and feet, then tossed them aside. Then he dragged her legs apart and looked at her pussy, watching her blush all over.

"Don't be embarrassed. This is where you get to show off your beautiful body."

"You're still clothed."

"I can fix that."

He unbuttoned his shirt, enjoying the way she watched him undress, the hunger in her eyes as she watched every button come undone until he shrugged out of his shirt. When he pulled the zipper down and dropped his pants, her eyes widened. He hurried through the rest of it, toeing off his shoes, then pulling off his socks and tossing everything into the front seat.

"Dear God you have a beautiful body."

He grinned. "Thanks. So do you."

She hesitated for a second, as if she wanted to deny his compliment, but then said, "Thank you."

"That's my girl." She started to reach for him, but he laid a hand on her shoulder and held her in place. "Stay where you are. I want to lick your pussy and hear you scream."

"Del. You make me crazy."

"That's the idea."

"Don't you want to..."

He smiled. "Oh, hell yeah. I'm going to fuck you, Janine. More than once tonight. I can't wait to get my dick inside your tight pussy. But first, you're going to come for me. Then after you're hot, wet, still quivering from your orgasm, I'm going to get you up on your hands and knees and pound my cock inside you until we both scream."

She spread her legs wide, clearly liking the plans he'd laid out for their evening. "Hurry."

Now she was talking. He slid onto his stomach and hooked his arms around her thighs, licking along the soft curve where her thigh met her buttocks. Janine lifted, then moaned when he moved his tongue around her swollen pussy lips. God, she was so wet already, her sweet juices pouring from her. What would it be like when she came? Would she flood his face? He could already imagine lapping up her cream as she forced his face into her cunt, desperate to continue the sensation of her climax. He wanted that for her.

Her pussy was bare except for a thatch of hair above her sex, giving him nothing but soft skin to play with. He licked from her cleft to her clit, swirling his tongue around the hood, then flattening it there. She liked it, because she shuddered and moaned and held onto the back of his head. He liked a woman who gave direction, even nonverbal. His cock, raging hard, was pressed between his body and the Navigator's carpet, and he rubbed against it. The friction was a turn on, reminding him that soon he'd be sheathed inside Janine's tight pussy.

And if the indications she gave him were right, it would be soon. She started to lift her hips, holding his tongue closer to her clit as she undulated. He let her direct the rhythm, and he licked around her button, then slid two fingers into her cunt.

"Oh, God, yes. Just like that."

Now they were getting somewhere. He withdrew, then plunged again, faster and faster, and licking with a rapid pace that made her thrash her body from side to side.

"I'm going to come, Del."

He murmured against her pussy and pressed his face closer, this time using his mouth to surround her clit and suck.

She cried out, shuddering as she lifted her hips against his face. Her pussy gripped his fingers in a tight hold and convulsed around them as she rode the rocking wave of climax. Finally, she relaxed, and he licked her with gentle swipes of his tongue, taking her down a notch until her breathing settled.

Del crawled over her and pressed his lips to hers, letting her take a taste of her own come.

She rubbed her finger over his lips, then brought his mouth to hers and kissed him deep, entwining her arms around him to pull him closer. The depth of her kiss spoke of emotion, of a thankfulness he didn't quite understand. Surely she'd been pleasured before. But maybe not well? If that was the case, he was more determined than ever to make this good for her.

But all thought fled from his mind, traveling straight to his dick when her soft fingers wrapped around his shaft and squeezed, then began to stroke.

"Janine." He moved to her throat, to the soft expanse of skin he'd glimpsed earlier when she'd tilted her head back to gaze at the stars. He kissed her there, lingering at the pulse point that pounded with a fast rhythm.

She played with his cock as if they had all the time in the world, tormenting his shaft with smooth movements. She swirled her thumb over the crest and he jerked in her hand, feeling the spill of hot precome. She took her thumb into her mouth and sucked, and he groaned in utter pleasure that she would be willing to taste him like that.

"My turn," she said. "Get out of the vehicle and stand."

Not so shy now, was she? He was more than happy to comply, anxious to see what she had in mind.

He slid out of the Navigator, his bare feet hitting a carpet of thick, cool grass. She climbed out after him and held onto his hands, then dropped to her knees. He looked to the heavens and thanked the stars for a perfect night and an equally perfect woman to spend it with.

Janine wrapped both hands around him, twisting them around his cock in an expert fashion that made his gut twist.

"Goddamn, Janine. That feels good."

"I watch a lot of porn," she said, her lips lifting in a wry smile. "I've always wanted to do that."

He laughed. She was amazing. Shy, yet honest and openly curious. He would imagine she didn't get to practice her moves on a lot of men. She didn't strike him as the experimental sort. If she was wary what people thought, she probably didn't often let loose. Except, maybe, with him?

He liked the thought of that.

"Play away. I'm all yours."

She did, capturing his cock between her lips and sliding her tongue around the seam. God, that drove him crazy. Now he could fulfill his fantasy, watching her lips surround him as she sucked him fully into her mouth, drawing him into the moist, hot cavern, all the way to the back of her throat.

Then she swallowed, squeezing his cockhead.

"Christ."

This was no inexperienced virgin, and if she got all this knowledge by watching porn, he'd have to thank the moviemakers, because she was a goddamn expert at it. She rolled her tongue over the head, then took him deep again, then all the way out to stroke him, sliding her hands over his saliva-drenched shaft. The combination of chilly breeze and her hot mouth was like cool heaven and blistering hell.

And speaking of hell, she dropped her hands, engulfing him again, licking and sucking him, obviously enjoying her play. Her mouth was like hellfire and he'd gladly stay there forever and take his punishment.

But when she cupped his balls, continuing to suck him into the vortex of her searing mouth, he knew he was either going to remain there and erupt, or something would have to change. And despite the pleasure he got from what she was doing, he didn't want to come in her mouth. Not this time.

"Enough." He pulled her to her feet and swept her into his arms, slanting his lips over hers. She clung to him, grasping his hair with greedy fingers that spoke of building need.

He deposited her back in the SUV, then climbed in after her, reaching over the front seat and fumbling through his jacket pocket until he found the foil packet. He tore it open and placed the condom on.

"On your hands and knees," he said, his hand already on her buttocks to hold her in place.

She positioned herself, craning her neck around to watch as he nudged her legs apart with his knee, then moved between her thighs. He placed his cock at her pussy, leaned back a little so he could see where their bodies met, then inched inside her.

So tight, her pussy lips spread like a molten welcome mat. Her heat even seeped through the condom. Janine tilted her head, her gorgeous hair spreading all over her back. He wound the soft waves around his fist and gave them a gentle tug as he seated himself fully inside her.

She gasped, then moaned, arching back to meet his thrusts.

A wind kicked up and blew into the back of the Navigator, cooling their heated bodies. Del drove deeper, then withdrew, each time tugging harder on Janine's hair. She responded with moans that let him know she liked what he was doing. Soon she was pushing back to meet each of his thrusts, shoving against his cock in a wordless request for more.

"That's it. Fuck me," he said, leaning back to watch her pussy swallow his dick.

The night was quiet, the only sounds the rustling trees and his cock slipping in and out of Janine's wet pussy.

"Can you hear me fucking you?" he asked.

"Yes."

"What if someone comes by and sees us?"

"I don't care. Fuck me harder."

She'd reached the point where she didn't care who saw them, where pleasure and sensation had taken over. Just where he wanted her, because he was at the same place. He let go of her hair and gripped her hips, digging his fingers into her flesh. He reared back and slammed into her, burying his cock to the hilt. His balls slapped against her, tightening, filling with the come he would soon spill. A bolt of lightning shot up his spine and he fought to control the rushing tide slamming against him.

"I want to feel you come around my dick, Janine. Touch yourself for me. Let me see it." He drew her up so her back was against his chest and clasped his arm around her waist, then started driving up and into her.

She reached down and covered her pussy with the palm of her hand. Fuck, that was hot, seeing her touch herself. He leaned over her shoulder and watched, listening to her draw panting breaths, then let out desperate moans as she brought herself ever closer to the finish. He knew that rush of sensation, could feel the blood pooling in his balls, the taut line stretching every nerve ending, and knew he was close.

"Come for me, here outside. Let me hear you scream. I want to know that you don't care who hears you."

"Yes. Yes, I'm going to come," she whispered, her hand moving in a rapid rhythm as she strummed her clit. She let her head rest on his shoulder, her body tensing. "Now, Del. I'm going to come now."

She stilled, bent her shoulders forward, then let out a cry that was the sweetest music he'd ever heard. It was loud and shuddering, her pussy tightening around him as her cream poured over his balls.

Del followed, groaning against her shoulder and neck as he jettisoned come over and over, pulsing out all he had until he was completely drained, physically and emotionally. He'd wondered exactly how to approach Janine, not sure how she was going to react to all this. She hadn't disappointed, in fact hadn't seemed at all reserved about being in public. She'd thrown herself full body into their play, had been everything he'd wanted, and more.

He knew there was a tigress lurking within the meek kitten.

He let go of Janine and she collapsed forward. He withdrew and took care of the condom, then crawled beside her, gathering her into his arms to stroke her hair and kiss her forehead.

It was then that she looked behind them and noticed the house.

"Oh, my God, Del. There's a house behind us."

"Uh huh."

"I didn't notice that when we drove up. What if someone heard us? What if they were watching us?"

He shrugged. "What if they did?"

"They could call the police. We should get out of here." She started to sit up, but Del held her tight in his embrace.

"Don't worry about it."

"Easy for you to say. You don't care about being caught in a compromising position." She pushed away from him and started to crawl out of the back of the SUV.

"You really have a hangup about this, don't you?"

Janine was already back in the passenger seat, grabbing for her dress. "I told you. I have a lot at risk here. God, I can't believe I didn't check our surroundings first. You make me lose my mind."

He slid off the tailgate and moved to the driver's seat, flinging his clothes into the back. "Lose your mind, huh? I'll take that as a compliment."

She slanted a glance in his direction. "You're going to drive naked?"

He turned the ignition, pressed a button on the center console and put the car in reverse. Janine looked over her shoulder as the garage door on the house behind them lifted.

Her eyes widened in panic. "Oh, shit! Someone's opening the door."

He flung his arm over the headrest and blew out a sigh. "Would you relax? I'm the one opening the garage door. The house   is   mine."

Chapter Five

Del made her feel like a dimwit. He could have told her the house was his before she'd launched herself into a full blown panic attack. Instead, he'd backed right into the garage with that smug smile of his plastered to his face.

Dickhead.

He'd pulled into the garage and they went inside to clean up a bit. His house was amazing. Two levels, though she'd only seen the downstairs. For some reason she expected modern, with chrome and leather everywhere. Instead, it was very warm and inviting, with cushiony sofas in the living room, fully stocked bookshelves and a huge picture window that overlooked the bluff where they'd made love. A fireplace stood off to the side of the room, and scattered everywhere were thick rugs that tickled her toes.

"Nice place," she said when she stepped out of the downstairs bathroom.

"Thanks."

She grabbed her dress and stepped into it. Del, who seemed quite comfortable wandering around naked, crossed his arms and arched a brow.

"What are you doing?"

"Getting dressed. It's time for me to go home. I have an early appointment tomorrow with some of the foundation members."

"Running, are you?"

"Of course not. I had a great time."

"And?"

She pulled the dress up over her bare breasts, grateful to be covered again. She felt...vulnerable when she was naked, especially since Del hadn't bothered to close the drapes on the living room window. "And what?"

He walked over to her and zipped up her dress. His fingers brushed her skin, the contact electric. The man was damaging to her senses. Not good. Not good at all. Being around him made her mind turn to mush, affected her judgment. "I'm not sure what you want from me, Del."

"What do *you* want, Janine?"

That was a loaded question. She'd like to pretend tonight hadn't happened, that she hadn't taken leave of her common sense and had an orgasm in a room filled with hundreds of people, that she hadn't had sex outside where anyone could have heard them, seen them. They might have even been followed.

"I just need to get home."

His fingers slipped away from her skin. "I'll get dressed and drive you back to the hotel."

She shivered at the loss of contact, then waited for him while he went upstairs and changed. When he came back down a few minutes later, he had on a pair of jeans and a cashmere sweater. Once again, he looked devastating. He was sexy no matter what he wore.

They drove back to the hotel in virtual silence. Janine suspected that Del had wanted her to stay the night, but she couldn't. This just wasn't going to work out. Being with Del made her uncomfortable, but not in the way she expected. She was out of her element—she was scared. Afraid, because she might enjoy this a little too much, like she could get used to this kind of fun. And this wasn't the kind of lifestyle she could lead. She knew she had to explain this to him.

"I had a wonderful time tonight, but the wild woman you're looking for isn't me."

"You underestimate yourself," he said, watching the road, not her.

"I can't afford to take risks like that. I have too much at stake."

This time he did glance at her. "You need to trust me. I'd never put your reputation in danger. Don't forget, I have as much to lose as you do. I run a legitimate business, yet I also manage to own a club that caters to sexual adventures. If I can pull it off without discovery, I think I can take care of your anonymity."

He made it sound so easy. Was it?

He pulled into the hotel parking garage and Janine directed him to her car. He parked next to hers and turned off the ignition, then half-turned in his seat to face her.

"It's up to you. I won't pressure or force you into doing anything you don't want to do."

She'd been staring down at her lap, at her hands that were so tightly clasped together her knuckles were white.

God, Janine. Relax. That had always been her problem. She never let go. Maybe it was time she did.

"I'm tempted."

"I like you tempted." He reached for a curling end of her hair and let it slide through her fingers. She met his probing gaze, mesmerized by his dark eyes.

"I enjoyed tonight. I would like to see you again, but if the press found out about what we were doing, if I was ever caught in the act, the foundation would suffer greatly."

"It won't happen."

"You don't know that for certain. You can't guarantee it."

He shrugged. "True enough. You'll just have to trust me."

That word again. How could she trust someone she barely knew? Of course she'd had no problem fucking him, and that required an element of trust, didn't it?

And she was tired of her staid, boring, safe life. Being with Del made her feel alive. She wanted this.

"Okay."

He cupped her cheek in the palm of his hand. "Okay, what?"

"We'll try this."

His half smile made her belly quiver. He leaned across the seat and brushed his lips across hers. Even that made her wet.

He got out of the SUV and moved around to her side, opened the door and helped her out, then slid his arms around her waist. She looked up at him, mesmerized by the dark promise in his eyes.

"Good. Now go get in your car, go home and get some rest, and do your work thing. I'll call you tomorrow."

She sighed. "Good night, Del."

He released her and waited until she had backed out of her parking space and pulled away. She watched him out of her rearview mirror, leaning against his vehicle, his arms crossed, a satisfied smile on his face.

She hoped she'd made the right decision. Somehow she felt like she'd just placed her future in Del's hands.

ಐ‍ಲ

They were dating. Honest to God dating. In public. It hadn't occurred to Janine that she could actually go out with Del in the normal sense, but of course she could. They didn't have to meet in clandestine fashion. Philippe Delacroix of Delacroix Motors was a great catch. The society page splashed pictures of them all over the place. Going out to dinner, attending theater and charity events together, any place where there was an event and she and Del went, they ended up having their picture taken.

And it was all on the up and up. Nothing sordid at all.

Del knew exactly how to manipulate the press. In fact, he was a master at it. Soon enough, she and Del being seen together was old news. Janine was in awe over the way he worked the media. And the great thing about it was the only thing the press saw was them as a couple. Dancing together, heads bent whispering, maybe holding hands, but other than that, everything was aboveboard and proper. Absolutely perfect.

But he'd been driving her crazy for the past two weeks, because that's all he'd been doing with her—escorting her to these public events, then taking her home. Dropping her off at her front doorstep, and giving her a chaste kiss goodnight.

What the hell was up with that? What about wild public sex? He hadn't even taken her back to Sneak Peek.

Had his interest in her waned after they'd had sex?

She was beginning to grow irritated. What kind of game was he playing? She wasn't the type of woman to throw herself at a man, so she hadn't asked him what was up or tried to make any moves on him. Besides, she really had enjoyed just going out with him. He was a wonderful date, they ran in many of the same circles and the press loved him. He was their golden boy—rich, successful, gorgeous and gave a lot of his money to charitable causes. In their eyes, he was above reproach.

Ha! If only they knew what he did in his private time. Though lately she'd wondered *who* he'd been doing in his private time, because it certainly hadn't been her. Then she'd mentally slap herself, because he'd been spending all his private time with her. And if she wasn't getting any, then he wasn't either. Or at least that's what she assumed.

Ugh. No wonder she didn't date much. So complicated.

Janine stared down at the paperwork on her desk, not at all interested in muddling through it. Her mind was occupied with all things Del. Honestly, she wasn't a teenager and shouldn't be spending her valuable work hours thinking about a man. Especially a man who was obviously becoming less and less interested in her—sexually, anyway. What an enigma he was.

"Janine, you have a call on line two. It's Del."

Her secretary sounded excited. Janine rolled her eyes. Everyone at the office was thrilled about her dating Del. He'd made a few appearances at the office and had the ladies charmed and drooling. Of course.

"Thanks, Fiona." She looked at the phone, deciding to make him wait for a few seconds, wondering what event he'd ask her to this time. Finally, she pressed the button and picked up. "Hi Del."

"Hey, gorgeous. What are you up to today?"

"Paperwork."

"Sounds boring. How about dinner tonight?"

She really should tell him no—play hard to get. Then again, she hadn't seen him in a few days and she was tired of being holed up in her house. "Sure. What did you have in mind?"

"There's a great new restaurant in Beverly Hills. La Belle Eau."

Brows raised, she said, "I've heard of it. Very exclusive."

"Yeah. It's been packed solid every night since it opened. I got us reservations at eight. Wear something sexy."

"Yes, master."

He laughed. "I have a surprise for you, too."

She arched a brow. "What kind of surprise?"

"You'll see. I'll be at your place at seven. See you then."

She hung up, then stared at the phone. A surprise. Good God, what could he possibly have in mind? Trepidation warred with excitement. Though she'd thoroughly enjoyed going out with him, she was ready for more, and was hoping his surprise tonight had something to do with the 'more' she was looking for.

With renewed enthusiasm, she tackled the paperwork on her desk. She wanted to leave work early today and prepare for tonight.

True to his word, Del arrived at seven with a gift bag in his hand.

"You look gorgeous," he said as he swept through her front door, pulled her into his arms and kissed her. Her breath caught at the feel of his lips pressed up against hers. Her body went into immediate overdrive—heating, pulsing, remembering what it felt like to be touched by him.

When he pulled away and she managed to catch her breath, she accepted the bag he held out.

"Thank you."

"Don't thank me yet," he said, his lips pulling into a wicked smile.

"Uh oh. Is it a ticking time bomb?"

"Maybe." He slid onto her couch. Dressed in black pants that looked impeccably tailored, a white shirt that hugged his well toned chest, finishing the look off with a dark jacket, he was once again utterly edible. She wished they were staying in tonight and having sex instead of going out.

Single-minded much, Janine?

She sat next to him and laid the gift bag on her lap, looked at it, then back at him.

"Go ahead. Open it. I promise nothing in there will bite you."

"Good to know." She reached in and pulled out the tissue paper, then looked in the bag. It was a pair of panties. Black panties. Satin, with lacy strings. Pretty. She pulled them out, but there was something different about them. The crotch was different. It was thicker, though there wasn't much to the crotch to begin with.

"What are these?"

She found out in a hurry when the panties moved in her hand. Or, rather, vibrated.

"Oh, my. How did that happen?"

Del pulled a tiny remote from his jacket pocket. "I did it."

"Are you serious? Remote control vibrating underwear?"

"Yes. Put them on."

"Now?"

"Of course. You're going to wear them to dinner."

To dinner. A new restaurant in Beverly Hills. One that no doubt would be solidly packed. It was Friday night after all.

When Del had mentioned the restaurant, she'd known right off which one he was talking about. Trendy, upscale, everyone had been talking about it for the two months it had been open. Janine figured she'd eat there after the buzz died down.

And speaking of buzz...

"You want me to wear these in public?" The thought of Del holding the remote to these panties in a public place was enough to make her face warm.

"Stand up, Janine."

Intrigued, she did.

"Spread your legs."

Del kneeled on the floor at her feet, tilting his head back to look at her. Her body flushed with heat when he skimmed his hands up her thighs and under her dress. He stopped at her hips and pulled her panties down. She shivered at the sensation of the material scraping her legs, of baring her pussy for him. She stepped out of the panties, then into the ones Del had bought for her.

"I can't believe I'm doing this."

"You're going to enjoy it." He took his time pulling the new panties over her hips, but didn't linger where she really wanted him to. In fact, he didn't even lift her dress up, just put the panties in place, smoothed her dress, then stood. "That should do it. Comfortable?"

She was, actually. Whatever battery was in there was covered by the padding within the panty. She nodded. "It's fine."

"Are you excited?"

"Dubious."

He snorted. "Trust me."

"Famous last words."

They drove to the restaurant and Janine kept waiting for him to push the remote controlling the tiny vibrator in the panties. He didn't, which only ratcheted up her anticipation as they pulled in front of the place. Del handed the keys to the valet so he could park the car, then held out his arm for her and they strolled inside.

There was a line outside, but Del bypassed it and walked straight to the desk and gave his name. They were seated right away, in a booth in the corner near the window.

La Belle Eau was gorgeous on the inside. Dark and romantic, with black and white place settings and crisp white tablecloths. And, as Del had mentioned, utterly packed. Waiters scurried from table to table seeing to the patrons' needs. She and Del had no more settled into their booth than their waiter arrived to take their drink order and present them with menus, citing the specials of the day. He brought their drinks right away and left them to linger over the menus.

"I can't believe you got us in here," she said, then took a sip of her cocktail.

He eyed her over his wine glass. "I know the owner. We went to school together in France."

"Ah, no wonder. It's a nice place and he seems to be doing well with it. I've heard people raving about it."

"He stayed in France after I left for the States. He went to the cooking school there. Graduated top of the class. His family were all chefs, too, so he comes from a good background. I think he'll make a go of it."

Their waiter came by and asked for their selection. Del brushed him off, said they wanted to enjoy their drinks for a while first. Janine couldn't help but squirm in her seat as she felt the pressure of her panties, wondering if Del had just been teasing her about using the remote in his pocket tonight.

Surely he wouldn't do that here, in this trendy, crowded restaurant. He hadn't yet, so maybe he was just teasing her. Just knowing she wore the panties and he held the remote was enough to moisten her and make her nipples hard.

"You're fidgeting."

Her gaze shot to Del. "I am not."

"Yeah, you are. Relax."

"I can't."

"Why not?"

"You know why not." She cast a look at his coat pocket.

"My jacket makes you nervous?"

She rolled her eyes. "You know what I'm talking about."

He tipped his glass and took a swallow of wine, but didn't answer her, which made her even more anxious.

He wasn't going to do anything. He'd just made her wear the panties to drive up her anticipation for later. Then, when they were riding in the car or stopped someplace and alone, he'd hit the remote and make her crazy. She finally let go of her anxiety and they talked about their week at work. The waiter came by and they ordered their meal and more drinks, and Del told her about a new delivery of cars that had come in earlier in the week.

She was listening until she felt a tiny buzz between her legs. It was so faint she was certain her mind had conjured it up, so she dismissed it while Del continued talking.

But there it was again, a pleasant tingle right in the vicinity of her clit. This time, the sensation lasted a few seconds longer. And she was certain she hadn't imagined it. She waited for it to stop, and when it did, she cast a questioning glance at Del, who smiled at her.

"Did you like that?" he asked.

"It was...interesting."

"But did you enjoy it?"

She shrugged, not wanting to give him any encouragement to continue. "It was okay."

The vibration intensified and her eyes widened. She froze until it stopped, then shuddered as the aftereffects of the pleasurable sensations continued to zing through her nerve endings. She leaned forward so no one could hear her whispering. "Del. Stop that."

He leaned back in his chair, an annoying smile gracing his handsome face. "Oh, I don't think so."

Again her panties started to vibrate, this time with more pronounced quivers. And it didn't stop. Janine began to pant as lightning pulses rolled across her clit. She felt it deep in her pussy and she fought back a moan. Her panties were moist and sticking to her skin. She cast a pleading look at Del.

"Relax, *bébé*."

Relax? She could come just like that, and he wanted her to relax? She gripped the edges of the table. Throbbing beats jetted between her legs—first slow, then fast. Harder, then softer, almost the same as if he were rubbing her there.

"Spread your legs for me."

He was making her crazy. She looked around, wondering if anyone noticed her squirming in her chair. But she did as he asked, widening her legs a little. He looked down at her spread thighs and smiled.

"No one's watching," he said. "But what if they were? Would you like that?"

"No." She was panting now as he drove up the vibration another notch. She shifted and the panties moved with her, adjusting the spot where they rubbed against her clit. "Oh, God."

She pressed back against the chair and lifted her hips, wanting to slide her hand between her legs and rub.

"Your cheeks are flushed."

Her gaze shot to his. "They are?"

He nodded, his lips curling upward in a smile she wanted to both slap and lick. She was irritated and turned on, and didn't know which was worse.

"You can deny with your words, but your body tells me the truth. You're enjoying this. I'll bet your panties are soaked."

He was whispering to her, leaning forward so only she could hear him. His lips touched her ear and she heard him inhale, then exhale, his warm breath caressing her neck.

"I can smell you, that sweet scent of aroused female. Did you know my dick is hard?"

He was killing her.

"I could take out my cock right now and jack off just thinking about the pleasure you're getting wearing those panties. You know the tablecloth at these tables goes all the way to the floor. My chair is against the wall. No one would even know."

Her gaze gravitated to his crotch. He slid his hand to his thigh, then over, lightly rubbing the telltale bulge in his pants. She bit back a groan and her panties flooded. When she looked up at him again, she sucked in her lower lip. In return, the vibration intensified.

"Del, please, don't do this to me."

"Oh, I'm going to do it to you. I want you to come for me, Janine. Right here, in front of all these people."

She shook her head, glanced over the crowd, then back at him. "I can't do this."

"You can. You want to. Let yourself go."

She was already so far gone, between the thought of how incredibly naughty and exciting this was, to the pleasure spiraling nearly out of control between her legs. Her heart pounded, her pulse raced, and her skin flushed with heat. Her breathing came in short bursts as she tried to ride out the incredible pulses soaring through her. She didn't know if she could fight them off without reaching down to rip off her panties. Now that would cause a scene—and that she didn't want.

"We're two lovers having an intimate dinner. No one is watching. Only you and I know that I'm giving you pleasure, that you're about to come all over those skimpy little panties."

The dark promise in his words only fueled the fire raging through her already stoked up senses.

"Imagine how sweet it will be to climax right here at the table, to know that you came in this trendy, full-to-capacity restaurant. Live out your fantasies, Janine. Come for me."

She couldn't fight the lure any longer. She turned to him, met his gaze, and as he increased the vibration and it soared across her swollen, sensitized clit, she climaxed.

She gripped his hand and squeezed. Her lips parted and she panted through an enormous orgasm, letting out a tiny moan as the rush of sensations poured through her. Del tilted his head and watched her, rubbing his hand over his cock as she shuddered through the aftereffects. She wished she could jump up right now and straddle him, impale herself over his cock. Her pussy throbbed with the need to feel him inside her.

"I really want to fuck you right now," he said. "My dick is so damn hard."

She was trembling, could still feel her pussy quaking from her climax.

Del kissed her lips, sliding ever so softly across her mouth, the tip of his tongue licking at hers.

"Damn, that was the hottest thing I've ever seen."

It was the hottest thing she'd ever done. He turned the vibrator off and she settled, trying to regain her composure.

Good timing, too, because the waiter approached bearing a tray with their food.

What if that had happened when she was in the throes of climax? The risks she took with Del were incredible. She lost her mind around him. She had to be more careful.

Then again, she'd just had a delicious orgasm, in public. She was living out her fantasies, just as he said.

She slanted a look at him. He smiled, nodded to her plate and winked.

"Enjoy your dinner, Janine."

Chapter Six

Del disengaged himself with as much delicacy as he could from the two women trying to wrap their bodies around him. He was also acutely aware of Ali's amused glance from across the crowded bar. He was going to take a ton of ribbing about this.

"As much as I'd love to ladies, I have a prior engagement this evening." He smiled and kissed each of their cheeks.

"Aww, Del, come on," Alicia said, affecting a pronounced pout. "We haven't played in too long. I thought we'd do the ménage room tonight."

Now that he'd untangled himself from the March twins' clutches, he breathed a sigh of relief, but still maintained the politeness his position as owner required. "You make it sound so tempting. But I already promised my evening to another."

"Some other time then?" Amy asked, thrusting her barely clad double D's out at him as if to say *surely you're not turning these down.*

"Definitely."

He'd barely turned on his heel before the luscious twins were swarmed by other guys wanting in on the action. They wouldn't be missing his attentions at all.

He strolled out of the bar, already knowing Ali would follow. By the time he reached the office, his partner was on his heels.

"You rejected the twins?" Ali asked, closing the door after him.

Del poured a drink, raised his brow and at Ali's nod, poured another. He handed it off. "Yes, I turned down the twins. What's wrong with that?"

"Nothing, other than I think you may have gone insane. Should I call a doctor? Do you have a fever?"

"Funny."

"Have you taken leave of your senses, my friend?"

"No. I have other plans for the evening."

Ali arched a dark brow. "With whom?"

"Janine."

"You've been seeing much of this woman. That is unusual for you."

"You monitoring my social calendar now? Are you reporting back to my mother in France?"

Ali snorted. "I don't think your mother would like what I would have to tell her about your social activities."

"Any more than yours would."

"Ah, but I have settled down now, remember?"

"How could I forget? You and Shanna parading around Sneak Peek, arms wrapped around each other, practically having sex in the lobby..."

"Now you're exaggerating."

"Am I? Our clients are starting to complain about all the exhibitionism."

Ali snorted. "Our clients would never complain about that. And love is very nice. You should try it sometime."

"I'm having too much fun just fucking around, but thanks. I think the two of you have enough love for the entire place."

"Famous last words. I never thought I would find love. But it found me. Perhaps the reason you are seeing so much of Janine, that you are even turning down the twins, is that love is knocking upon your door."

Del rolled his eyes. "Now you *are* starting to sound like my mother. Are you sure she hasn't called you?"

Ali laughed. "I think you are trying to change the subject. You feel something for this woman."

"Yeah, I do. She makes my dick hard."

"Ah. Denial. I remember the feeling. You do it so well."

Del took a long swallow, letting the alcohol burn its way down his esophagus before answering. "I'm not denying she makes my dick hard."

"You are avoiding the subject of love."

"I don't love her. I just like fucking her."

"We shall see what happens, won't we?"

Now it was Del's turn to shake his head. "I think love has ruined you. I might have to find a new partner."

Ali stood, ignoring Del's teasing. "I think your downfall is inevitable. The fact you have spent almost a month exclusively with this woman, you haven't engaged any other woman at the club since the night you met Janine, and you even walked away from the twins tonight, is very telling. Very telling indeed."

Sometimes he hated that his friend and partner knew him so well. "Go play with your fiancée, Ali."

Ali waggled his brows. "I intend to. Have fun with Janine. Someday soon I intend to say 'I told you so'."

After the door closed behind him, Del stood and turned to the mirror behind his desk.

Love. No way. Not him. He wasn't ready for that whole settling down thing yet. Hell, he might never be ready. His life was perfect the way it was. Why change it? He enjoyed a multitude of women, none of them ever pressured him for a commitment, and the thought of spending the rest of his life with just one woman had always made his stomach clench.

Not that he had any problem with marriage. His parents had a great one. They loved each other and had made great role models for happily ever after. And when he was done being single, he'd get married, do the whole kids and white picket fence thing.

When he was ready.

But so far no one woman had given him that urge.

The intercom on his desk buzzed, rescuing him from thoughts of love and marriage. He leaned over and pushed the button. "Yeah."

"Del, Janine is here."

He smiled. "Thanks, Steve. Send her into my office."

Aware of his jacked-up pulse and the rush of adrenaline that had hit him as soon as Steve announced Janine had arrived, Del shook his head. Yeah. She didn't affect him much, did she?

Maybe he was in denial, and Janine had come to mean more to him than he thought. He hadn't even realized that he'd stopped seeing other women since the night he'd met her, that he hadn't had sex with anyone but her. More importantly, that he hadn't *wanted* to fuck any woman but her.

Ah, hell. He dragged his hand through his hair and pondered what it meant, if anything. Maybe it meant nothing at all and he'd let his conversation with Ali affect him.

She knocked on the door and he shook his head. He walked over and opened it, grinning at her. "You don't need to knock, babe."

She looked up at him through her dark lashes. "You might have been in a meeting."

"Always so polite, aren't you?" He held the door open and she walked in. "And you look like a knockout tonight."

He loved the way the color hit right away on her high cheekbones. "Thank you. So do you."

He was wearing jeans and a polo shirt. Hardly anything special. On the other hand, she wore a short black skirt and a tight, body-hugging top, meant to show off her killer curves. The shoes had at least three inches on the heel, making her tanned, shapely legs look even longer than they were. Men's tongues must have been hanging all over the hallways as she made her way to his office. He liked the thought of that, because tonight she belonged only to him.

"My dick's getting hard already."

She laid her purse on his desk, tilted her head and glanced at his crotch. "Is it?" She strolled toward him, slung one arm around his neck and planted her palm against his hardening cock, then smiled. "So it is."

When she began to rub her hand up and down against him, he wrapped his arm around her and jerked her closer. "Be careful."

"Why?"

"Because I don't have much patience tonight."

"So, what you're saying is that you want me. Right now."

"Yes."

She squeezed his shaft. "And that you're not in the mood to play games."

"No, I'm not."

"You want to fuck me."

"Yes."

She tilted her head back, her lips parted, her eyes drifting partway closed in a way he found oh so sexy. "Then do it."

"I want others to watch us fuck."

Her brows lifted. He waited for her to object, but she shrugged. "Whatever you want. I just want your cock inside me. I'm wet, my pussy's hot and I need to come."

He'd already had the scene set up, but she'd somehow taken control. Or rather, taken his self-control. He'd planned a slow seduction, to take his time with her. Obviously, Janine had ripped away his senses and there was no time for foreplay. She was ready. And so was he.

Her lips were parted, her breathing shallow. He covered her mouth and she opened for him, sliding her tongue in to lick at his. He groaned, and she reciprocated with a whimper, grasping his hair and tugging to signal her demand for more. He felt her need and it mirrored his own, ratcheting up his desire to a quick frenzied pitch. There was a wild hunger inside her and he intended to satisfy it.

He took her hand and led her from the room, a short trip down the hall and into another room. He closed and locked the door behind him. This room was similar to his office, except it was devoid of almost all furniture. An easy chair in the corner was the only furnishing. A small room, the only adornment was a full mirror along one wall and lush, thick carpet under their feet.

Del pulled Janine toward the mirror, placing her in front of it, then pushed a button to the side of the mirror. The lights went out and the mirror reflected the other side. A man and a woman stood in another room. No other people were in the room.

The woman was striking, with long, straight raven hair that fell almost to her buttocks. The man was tall, muscular, his skin dark and gleaming in the overhead lights. Del had chosen the couple not only because of their adventurous spirit, but also because he thought Janine might find them both appealing.

They were both naked and stood in front of the mirror, staring back at Del and Janine.

"Rose and Joaquin are here for our pleasure tonight," he explained. "They can see and hear us, just as we can see and hear them. They're friends of mine and very discreet, so you don't need to worry about anything."

"So they *can* see us."

"Yes, we can," Joaquin said, his hand on Rose's shoulders. "You are very beautiful, Janine. But you are still clothed." Joaquin looked to Del. "She needs to be naked."

Rose smiled as Joaquin's hands drifted down and swept over her breasts. Del heard Janine's rush of indrawn breath.

Del mirrored Joaquin's movements, moving his own palms over Janine's breasts.

"You're right. This would be much better on Janine's soft skin." He slid his palms further down, stopping at the hem of her top, then drew it upward. Janine lifted her arms and Del pulled the top over her head. She didn't have a bra on.

"So sexy," he whispered against the side of her head, then let his thumbs drift down over her nipples.

Janine didn't say a word. Nor did she tilt her head back to look at him. Her gaze was riveted on Rose and Joaquin, to the way Joaquin's large hands covered Rose's small breasts, the way his thumb and forefingers grasped Rose's dark nipples and pinched.

"Oh, yes, Joaquin," Rose said, her eyelids drifting closed. "Harder."

Janine shuddered.

Del stepped back and drew the zipper down on Janine's skirt, then bent down and pulled the skirt to the floor. He held onto her hand while she stepped out of the skirt.

"No panties either." His woman had come dressed for sex tonight. He swept his hands along her ankles, moving upward along her calves, her knees, her thighs, breathing in her musky scent as he stood.

"You must undress too," Rose said, her gaze on Del. "I want to see your hard cock."

This was going to be fun.

Janine couldn't breathe. She was on definite sensory overload. Between Rose and Joaquin—they had such incredible bodies, and their sexual chemistry was overwhelming—plus having Del behind her, she might just self combust.

Now Janine did a half turn to watch Del. He stood and pulled his polo shirt off and cast it into the chair in the corner. His eyes darkened and he quirked a smile as he kicked off his shoes, then drew the zipper down on his jeans. When he tugged them down, his cock sprang out, hard and pressing up against his belly. Janine's eyes widened with pleasure.

He moved forward and turned her around to face the mirror. His cock pressed against her buttocks, thick and hard and she swore she could feel it pulsing. God, she wanted it in her. Now.

"Yes," Rose said, then licked her lips. "You are more than ready for fucking."

"You like his cock?" Joaquin asked.

Rose nodded.

"You want to watch him fuck his woman while I do you tonight?"

Joaquin's fingers disappeared behind Rose. Janine saw them slip between Rose's legs, then between her pussy lips. Rose gasped as Joaquin finger fucked her. Janine's pussy quivered as if she could actually feel the sensation.

She nearly cried out as Del's hand slid between the cheeks of her ass, his warm fingers searching her pussy lips. She kept her focus on Rose's pussy, desperately seeking what she saw. When Del slid two fingers into her pussy, she cried out. Being able to see it, to feel it at the same time, was phenomenal.

"Is she wet?" Joaquin asked.

"Dripping," Del answered.

"Let me see."

Del turned her, guided her so her back was to the mirror. Janine was so turned on she felt dizzy.

"Bend over, baby."

Oh my God. Her ass was nearly pressed up to the mirror. She bent down, aware that Joaquin was looking directly at her pussy, could see her anus, could see Del's fingers buried inside her, fucking her hard and fast. She should be mortified, but the only emotion she could summon was pure exhilaration. She'd never been so excited.

"Suck my cock, Rose."

"You'll want to watch this," Del said. He withdrew his fingers and pulled her upright, turning her around so she could see.

Rose dropped to her knees and placed her full lips around Joaquin's cock. Her tongue darted out, licking the underside of his shaft. Then his shaft began to disappear, her throat undulating as she swallowed him like a python. Joaquin held the back of her head, forcing her to take more and more of him, a look of utter ecstasy on his face.

Janine glanced over at Del. He had fisted his cock and was stroking it as he watched Rose and Joaquin. Dear God it was hot watching him masturbate.

"Fuck her," Joaquin said to Del, his voice thick with arousal. "I want to see her face. I want to see your cock going in and out of her while I fuck Rose."

Joaquin pulled Rose in front of him and faced her toward the mirror. Del did the same, placing Janine as a—ironically enough—mirror image to Rose. Then he moved behind her. He nudged her legs apart and caressed her buttocks as he spread them, positioning her where he wanted her. It was as if she were watching a choreographed dance, both parties moving in tandem, making almost exactly the same moves. It really was like watching Del and herself in a mirror, but with the thrill and excitement of being able to see another couple have sex. Rose's gaze met hers and Janine saw in Rose's eyes the glittering pleasure sizzling through her own body.

Del wrapped one arm around her waist and moved up behind her, his cock nudging her sex. Her body throbbed in response to the heat of his body against her, to the soft head of his cock sliding with a teasing caress between her wet folds. She wanted him inside her, wanted to feel the pressure, the thrust, that feeling of being filled by him.

"Are you ready?" Joaquin looked at Del.

"Now."

Del thrust, burying his cock inside her. Janine jumped, startled by the sudden invasion, then melted as her walls surrounded him. Heat fused her from her feet up to her neck, the pinpricks of goose bumps raising on her skin despite the warmth of the room.

Rose's eyes widened as, at the same time, Joaquin drove inside her. She leaned back against Joaquin, giving Janine a view of his shaft moving between her spread pussy lips. Rose's face showed rapture.

Janine knew what that felt like as Del speared her with plunging strokes. Deep, hard, he held her tight against him and thrust to the hilt, then eased almost all the way out. Now it was her turn to palm the glass mirror, touching her hands where Rose's were, as if they held onto each other for support.

"Do you like watching them fuck?" Del asked her, his voice tight with strain as he tunneled up inside her with slow, deliberate movements.

"Yes."

He bent down, pulling her back against him now, tilting her hips forward. His hand found her clit and began to rub in unhurried, gentle motions.

"Spread your legs, baby. Let Rose and Joaquin see what I'm doing to you."

She couldn't stand this. Being able to see and to feel was sensory overload. Joaquin lifted Rose in his powerful arms, and onto his cock, then thrust upward again, repeating the motions. She held onto his arms and rode him, tilting her head back and moaning. His cock was wet with her pussy juices, her sex swollen from his punishing thrusts. Finally, she slid her hand down and rubbed her clit, her eyes locked on Janine. Her lips were parted, her breasts rising and falling with her labored breaths.

As her moans grew louder, Janine knew Rose was close to letting go. Janine felt her own spasms like an oncoming train, and she could do nothing to hold them back.

"I'm coming!" Rose cried, shuddering in Joaquin's arms. Joaquin grimaced and pumped like a madman against her.

Janine felt her own body tightening with impending climax. She wanted to come, too, wanted her completion in tandem with Rose's. Del pressed harder against her clit, increased his thrusts, and she burst into orgasm, gripping his arm and digging her nails into his skin. Sensation rushed through her and she cried out, closing her eyes as Del tensed against her. Now it was just the two of them and she let the ecstatic agony soar through her nerve endings. Her entire body shook with the force of the convulsions. Del wrapped both his arms around her and held her, groaning against her neck as he pulsed inside her with his own climax.

They were both panting, Del's hot breath ruffling her hair against her cheek. She couldn't speak, didn't even want to look at the couple in the other room. Del withdrew and turned her around to face him, planting his lips on hers in a soul shattering kiss. He kissed her with depth, with surprising emotion, pulling her as close to him as he could get. When they finally came up for air, he lifted her into his arms, moved to the button on the mirror and pushed it. The room went dark. The mirror image disappeared and Del slid down to the floor with her still nestled in his embrace.

She smoothed her hands over his sweat-dampened skin, pressed kisses to his chest, his neck, the side of his mouth, feeling his heart return to normal under her palm.

"You okay?" He smoothed his hand across her damp hair.

"Yes, I'm fine." She loved that he cared enough to ask.

"How about we get dressed and go back to my place."

She leaned back, searching his face, though the room was so dark she couldn't see a thing. "Do you have something in mind?"

"Yeah. You. Me. Alone. This scene was great, but I'm ready to have you to myself."

She smiled in the darkness, and her heart swelled with an emotion she couldn't identify. But it made her warm from the inside out. "What a great idea."

Chapter Seven

The Bartolino Foundation's horse race for charity was one of the biggest outdoor fundraisers of the year, and always left Janine a nervous wreck. It was highly touted, and since it was southern California, well attended by a horde of celebrities. And that meant tons of publicity. Camera lights had been shining all day and flashbulbs had already popped so often in her face she was afraid she was going to be rendered permanently blind. And her smile was permanently frozen to her face. But the ticket sales were through the roof and the press the foundation was going to get out of this would be tremendous. She made a mental note to suggest public relations staff get a bonus this year. They had really outdone themselves for this event.

Tramping around dirt and hay in a skirt and heels though, now that was difficult. But she wanted to personally thank the sponsors, the horse owners and everyone who had agreed to participate. Which was time consuming, but necessary. She'd been so busy she hadn't seen Del since they arrived at the race track together this morning, which had been approximately seven hours ago. He'd helped her out so much, acted as a fantastic host, even taking on responsibility for entertaining some of the blue haired ladies, who found him absolutely charming as he led them to their box seats.

Del, charming. Imagine that. Lethally charming, in fact, and she was afraid he'd charmed her heart right away from her. These past few weeks she hadn't held onto her guard. She'd let go, lived the kind of life she'd only dreamed about. Oh, sure. She'd gone into this thinking it was a fun sexual adventure, never knowing she was going to lose her heart in the process.

Del was everything she could ever want in a man. Gorgeous, intelligent, fun to be with, successful, a wonderful companion and without a doubt the best sexual partner she'd ever had. She'd been living out her fantasies in ways she'd never expected. But every day she spent with him left her in agony, because she wanted more. He was a drug in her system, and she had no idea how this was going to end up.

Surely they had no future together.

Or did they? He seemed fine with the way things were at the moment, but as far as she knew he could be seeing ten other women. Though she wouldn't know since she'd never asked him. And she knew why she'd never asked, because she didn't want to know the answer.

Coward. He'd spent every night with her for the past two weeks. Either he had the stamina of a bull or they were officially a couple. Or were they? She didn't know what they were. Officially or unofficially. She should stop worrying about it and just enjoy the time they spent together.

Why did she have to angst over everything?

She headed into the dark barn, enticed by the cool air and the smell of fresh hay. She loved horses, always had, though she didn't get to ride as often as she used to. The sounds of the animals in the barn always drew her. Besides, she felt the need to get away for a few minutes and catch her breath before going back out there. Surely she could take five minutes before someone needed her for something, couldn't she?

She wandered the length of the barn and admired the horseflesh. No one else was in there, fortunately, allowing her the time to herself. She stopped at the stall of a beautiful chestnut, who stuck his head out and inspected her.

"Aren't you just the prettiest thing in here?" she said, wanting to run her hand over his beautiful coat, but knowing better.

"No comparison. You're prettier."

She whirled at the sound of Del's voice, then on instinct walked into his arms. He kissed her with a fierceness that made her heart kick up. He tightened his hold around her and lifted her off the ground. When he released her lips and set her down, she was out of breath, her body warm and needy. Being with him was like an instant turn on. Just having him in her sights made her body temperature rise, her pulse kick up, her breasts swell.

So this was desire. She'd never felt it like this for another man, this instantaneous rush of arousal. It was a unique, heady experience.

"I've missed you today," she admitted.

"I've been entertaining your guests," he said with a smile.

"So I've noticed. And thank you."

"My pleasure. Another successful charity event, I see."

She nodded. "I hope so."

He slid his knuckles across her cheek. "Quit worrying."

"It's what I do best," she said, allowing a faint smile.

He walked her backward, between two stalls. "No, it's not what you do best. I know where you excel."

Her body went from warm to red hot in an instant, already knowing what he had in mind. She didn't know if the rush of heat coursing through her was excitement or utter terror. "Del, not here. Not now."

His brows arched in that devilish way that never failed to make her panties wet. "Like I said, you worry too much. Quit thinking about everyone else and start thinking about yourself and what you want. You want a quickie, knowing thousands of people are out there and could walk in here."

"No. I'm working."

He kept moving. Her back hit the wall of the barn.

"Five minutes. My dick's already hard. I want to be inside you, fucking you, my dick moving in and out of your wet pussy. You are wet, aren't you?"

Her pussy quivered, moistened. God, the way he got to her, excited her. The thought of doing it here in the barn, just as he described... "Damn you, Del."

"That means yes." She only caught a glimpse of his triumphant smile before he covered her lips with his, his tongue sliding inside her mouth and searching for hers. Intense, demanding, just like his hands moving over her body. He lifted one of her legs and positioned it over his hip, then unzipped his pants. Everything was hurried, a rush of whispers and tangled bodies. Janine drank it all in...the danger, the thrill, and how it made her nipples hard, straining against her satin bra.

"Hurry. Fuck me. I need you inside me now."

"Christ." He gave her what she asked for, pulling her panties to the side and shoving his cock inside her with one hard thrust. She fought back a scream and bit down on her bottom lip as he pumped his cock inside her with furious, solid strokes. And every time he thrust himself fully inside her, he'd grind against her clit.

She wasn't going to last. Her pussy gripped his shaft and ripples sailed through her. She felt like she was climbing through a spinning vortex.

"Baby, let go," he whispered, his fingers digging into her ass cheeks as he tilted her pelvis toward him, pushed in and ground against her, circling his pelvis around her clit.

She held onto his shoulders and buried her face against his chest, holding back the torrential cry as she climaxed, shaking and shuddering. God, she wanted to scream at the intensity of the sensations, but she couldn't. But Del groaned, coming in a hard burst inside her, his body trembling too.

Out of breath, she could only hold onto him, their faces buried together as they hid in the dark corner of the barn.

That's when the photographer snapped their picture. She heard the popping sound, saw the flash of lights, but she kept her face averted, not knowing what else to do as the photographer snapped one, two, three photographs. Then she heard the sound of pounding footsteps as he ran.

Too stunned to move, Janine stayed frozen.

"Fuck!" Del swore. "I'll go after him."

Janine held tight to Del's arm, panic tightening her throat. Then reality struck. "Don't. I don't want him to see us. I don't want anyone to see us. It's bad enough everyone will by tomorrow."

They disengaged, righting their clothing in a hurry. Del pushed back, looking at her.

Janine didn't know what to do, what to say. Someone had just taken their picture, while Del's cock was still inside her. At a charity fundraiser for the Bartolino Foundation. Shame washed over her at the thought of how she'd disgraced her father's company. Why, why did she let Del talk her into this? She knew better. Not here and not now. Why didn't she push

239

him away and say no? There were other times, other places, for this kind of fun. This one had disaster written all over it and she should have listened to that tiny voice inside her head telling her it had been a bad idea.

She shook her head, unable to find the words to describe the impending devastation. Tears pooled in her eyes, but she held them back. The last thing she needed was to fall apart in public.

"My staff will be looking for me," was all she could manage, her voice the barest of whispers. "I should go."

She pushed past Del.

"Janine." He grasped her arm, stilled her.

She turned, looked up at him, refusing to acknowledge the shock and misery on his face. He couldn't possibly feel as bad as she did about this. He was a man. Men lived for this. He ate up this kind of lifestyle, this thrill. "Don't."

"I'm so sorry, babe. I'll fix this."

He looked as miserable as she felt. And yes, she wanted that, wanted to throw herself into his arms, burst into tears and handle this with him. She wanted to walk out with him, finish her day and then go home with him tonight and figure this out together. But that's not how her life worked, that wasn't how she had been taught to deal with problems. Besides, he didn't understand the impact this would have on the foundation. She'd have to work this out on her own.

"You can't." She shrugged, not knowing what else to say. "It's done. We're done."

He frowned, as if he didn't understand what she'd just said. "You don't mean that. I really can take care of this. Trust me."

His words called to mind something he'd said when they first met. Her blood boiled. Everything rushed at her at once and she couldn't hold back the tidal wave of emotion, lashing out at the only person standing there to take it. She tilted her head back to meet his gaze. Ignoring his pleading eyes, she said, "Trust you? Trust. You. That worked out so well for me, didn't it? I did trust you, Del, and now my picture is going to be splashed all over the society page tomorrow, in the midst of a sex act in this barn, with you. I should have said no when you suggested it, and I didn't. Now my stupid decision is going to cost the foundation its reputation."

She pushed away from him, shaking her head as she paced back and forth. "I'm so incredibly stupid. I need to walk away from this before I sink in any deeper, before I can't get out of it. It's over, Del."

"Janine—"

She held out her hand. "Please don't. We're not good for each other. This isn't working. I should have never done anything with you. I was fine before I met you."

He crossed his arms, his gaze narrowing. "Were you? You were miserable and lonely."

"I was happy. You don't know me."

"Now you're lying to yourself."

"Don't presume to tell me how I feel. You've already presumed, and assumed, way too much about me. But I'll give you this much—the mistake was mine and it was a big one. I don't belong with you. Your lifestyle isn't one I can live with, so I'd appreciate if you'd stay the hell away from me."

His lips were set in a tight line. Now he was angry. Oh, that was funny, considering he had nothing to lose and she was about to lose everything. Before she really caused a scene, she walked out of the barn, determined not to think about all of this until later. Right now the foundation needed her to be strong, and the foundation was all that mattered.

She'd promised her father she'd take care of it. Dammit!

Too bad she hadn't been thinking about the foundation when she decided to take Del up on his offer of fun and games. She'd made a vow to run the foundation the same way he always had, keeping its reputation clean and above reproach.

She'd failed. The one and only thing her father had counted on her for, and she couldn't live up to his expectations. Because she'd fallen in love with the wrong man, and because of that had made all the wrong decisions.

Her heart tore in two. On one side stood her father and the foundation, what they stood for, everything the Bartolino family had always been. On the other side stood Del; the excitement and warmth she'd grown to love experiencing from him. How could she walk away from him, from everything he'd shown her? He'd given her a new life, a chance to become the woman she'd always known she could be. If only she'd been a little more cautious...

Water under the bridge. She hadn't been careful enough. Now she had to live with the consequences. Tears came again, and she blinked them back, wanting to slide down against the barn wall and sob. God, she was miserable, missed Del already. Why couldn't she just fall apart, why couldn't she have let him help her?

Because she realized no one could help her. Not even Del. Distance was the best way. Apart, they could both weather this through. Together it would be a nightmare.

She put on her sunglasses and plastered on a smile as a couple of the committee members headed her way.

She'd fall apart when she got home.

"What crawled up your ass today?"

Del snapped his gaze toward Ali, who leaned casually against the doorway to his office. "Nothing. I'm working out a problem."

"What kind of problem?"

He inhaled, blew it out, then said, "Shut the door."

Ali stepped in and Del filled him in on the happenings at today's horse show. By the time he was finished, Ali's expression was grave.

"That is very bad news, my friend," Ali said. "What can you do about it?"

"Not sure. But I can't let those photographs come out tomorrow. Janine will be ruined."

Ali leaned back in the chair. "Will she be recognized from the photographs?"

Del shrugged. "Not sure."

"What about you?"

"I don't care about me, you know that. Hell, it would be great press for the club. But I can't let this happen to Janine. It's my fault." Fuck. Sometimes he took too many chances. He shouldn't have done it, shouldn't have put Janine in that position.

Sometimes he really was a dick.

Ali arched a brow. "You never cared about a woman's reputation before. You've always made it clear that what you do with a woman is consensual, and if you're caught in public that's just the way it is."

"I've never cared—" He stopped himself before he completed the sentence, but the words had already tumbled out.

"You love her."

"Shit." With a sigh, Del nodded. "Yeah, I guess I do."

"Why?"

"Why?" He'd never thought about why before. Hell, he'd never realized he loved her until just this moment. "Because she's beautiful, intelligent, capable, she runs a successful corporation and loves giving to the less fortunate, she's sexy as hell and I think she's fearless. Though she doesn't realize that last part yet."

Ali grinned. "You sing her praises well. Can I say 'I told you so' now?"

"Help me solve this problem and you can say it every day for the rest of our lives."

"That's an offer I don't wish to refuse. The first thing you need to determine is if the photographer has pictures of your faces."

Del thought for a moment, trying to remember the moment when the flashes of light went off. Hell, that was kind of hard to do considering he'd just had an orgasm, was spent and panting, his face buried in Janine's neck.

He sat up, wracking his brain, remembering positioning. "No, he didn't. My face was in Janine's neck, and her face was buried on my shoulder. No way did he get our faces in those shots he took."

"That's very good. So the only thing he has is your bodies entangled. But no proof as to who you are. You can deny it."

Del wrinkled his nose. "Yeah, we could, but not my preference. I'd rather do something else."

"Such as?"

He thought about it for a few minutes, then remembered who had been at the charity horse race today. But would she go for it? As much as she loved publicity, it would still be a huge risk.

Of course she would. He grinned and looked at Ali. "I have a great idea."

He picked up the phone.

Chapter Eight

Janine didn't want to open her drapes, afraid to see the first rays of dawn seeping through, signaling the end of life as she knew it.

"Dramatic much, Janine?" She rolled her eyes, stood and moved to the coffeemaker, refilling her empty cup. She'd tried to sleep, but hadn't managed more than tossing from one side of the bed to the other. Quiet crying, wishing Del was there with her, which only made her feel more miserable and led to even more insomnia. Anxiety had won and she'd finally crawled out of bed at three in the morning to make coffee. Pacing while standing seemed much more effective.

After the horse race ended yesterday, she'd met with her staff, debriefed, then told her assistant something urgent had come up and she would need to reschedule all her appointments for the following day. Not that anyone would want to meet with her after the pictures appeared in the newspaper, anyway, but she figured she might as well do it in advance and save herself at least a little humiliation.

She glanced up at the clock. Six a.m. The newspaper would be arriving shortly. With a heavy sigh, she trudged upstairs and into the bathroom, took a shower, then did her hair and makeup and walked into her closet to choose an appropriate outfit. Reporters would show up soon enough and she wanted to be presentable when they did. She dressed in a pair of black slacks and a cream sleeveless top, hoping to look respectable.

Respectable. Ha. That term would never be associated with her again.

Why had she taken Del up on his offer in the first place? She'd lived thirty years of her life without ever living out her fantasies, and in the space of a few weeks had completely deviated. As she put on her earrings, she looked at herself in the mirror, remembering every intimate detail of what she and Del had shared.

Warm pleasure mixed with mortification. Her heart wrapped around thoughts of Del even as her mind tainted everything they'd done. No matter what her heart wanted, she should have never besmirched the family name with her sick, perverted fantasies.

Visuals of everything she and Del had shared together entered her mind. The night of the charity ball, then outside in his SUV. At the restaurant, at Sneak Peek, so many others. Even just times they shared alone. Every single episode played through her head like a movie, each scene vivid and evoking heated passion and playful fun. What was wrong with a little harmless sex? Had they hurt anyone doing what they did? What they'd shared was between the two of them and no one else, meant for their pleasure alone.

She crossed her arms, then shook her head, frowning at her reflection. No. Her fantasies *weren't* sick and perverted. She was normal. She'd had feelings for Del. And dammit, he'd had feelings for her, too. Their relationship had been leading somewhere beyond just fun exhibitionism and voyeurism.

Hadn't it? Or had she conjured all that up in her own head? Del had made her no promises other than wild and crazy sex. Had she read more into their relationship? Had she foolishly fallen in love with him, and her feelings hadn't been reciprocated?

What did it matter anyway? It was over. She'd made it clear to him yesterday in the barn. God, had she made it clear. She blinked back tears remembering that conversation, at the way she'd treated him as if this had been all his fault.

She missed him, wished she could talk to him right now.

Yeah, she wasn't conflicted much. She'd pushed him away and now she wanted him back. He was probably glad to be rid of her. And it was probably for the best, anyway. They were ill-matched, had been from the beginning. Great chemistry did not make a forever match.

So why did she feel so damn miserable? Disgusted with herself, she turned away from the mirror and slipped on her watch and a bracelet. No other adornment. Keep it simple. Then she walked downstairs, thoughts pummeling her head nonstop.

Her father would never have forgiven her. Thank God he wasn't alive to see what was going to happen to the foundation. She'd resign, of course, and turn over the reins to her vice chairman. She didn't look forward to having that meeting with the board of directors, having to explain her actions. Nausea rose, but she fought it down.

The foundation would be in good hands, would continue to run smoothly. They would weather this scandal, with her stepping down as soon as possible.

She fought back tears, tired of crying, refusing to feel sorry for herself anymore. She looked down at her watch.

Six thirty. The newspaper was probably at the front door. Her stomach clenched in an agonizing knot, but she had never been the type to avoid the inevitable. She strolled to the door and opened it, afraid reporters would already be amassed and ready to snap her picture, bombard her with questions.

No one was there yet to snap her picture. But the newspaper awaited her, glaring up at her with a sickening finality. She swallowed, bent down and retrieved it, then shut and locked the door, turning around and leaning against it. She took a minute to calm her raging heartbeat, catch her breath, then opened the paper, discarding everything with the exception of the section containing the society pages. With ruthless intent she flipped open the pages, sliding down the door to sit on the floor. Her legs shook so much she couldn't stand any longer.

She spread the pages open, her gaze scanning every picture. There was the charity horse race with corresponding photographs. She felt dizzy, her breaths coming in too fast now. Hyperventilating was a really bad idea, so she mentally slowed down each breath. Panic wasn't going to help her anyway, couldn't avoid the inevitable.

She looked. Looked again. Read the article. Nothing about her and Del. Only the work of the foundation, the success of the charity horse race, how much money had been raised and pictures of a few of the celebrities in attendance.

That was it.

That was it?

What the hell? She dropped the paper and stared straight ahead, not understanding.

Where were the pictures of her and Del? The photographer had taken them and run. He had to want to use them for—

Then it hit her. Of course. Dread made her stomach feel as if lead had been dropped in there. He hadn't sold the photographs to the main newspaper. He'd sold them to the tabloids.

Oh, God.

She managed to stand, her legs even shakier than before, kicked the newspapers out of the way and hurried into the kitchen, grabbing her keys.

She had to know, had to see them.

This was going to be oh so much worse. The society page in the newspaper was bad enough, but to be in the tabloids? It was so sordid.

Clutching her stomach, she went to the garage, hit the button to lift the door and started her car, hurrying down the driveway. Okay, where to find them? Her brain wasn't working! She had to think. She didn't buy the damn things, where were they?

Tabloids would be on sale at the grocery store down the road. She remembered seeing them there. The new weekly issues should be there this morning. Would it even be there? Of course it would. This was news, scandal even. Panic striken, she drove the short distance and parked, tossed on her sunglasses and sauntered into the store, zooming into the magazine aisle.

There were at least seven tabloids there. All she did was glance at the titles of the magazines. She didn't even look at them, just grabbed one copy of each and went to the express checkout lane, hoping her face wasn't plastered across the front page of any of them. She purposely kept her head down and paid cash. After she checked out, she went to her car and pulled them all out of the bag, scanning the covers.

There, in one of the sleazy, best-selling rags, was her picture. It was grainy and dark, but was her and Del, embracing in the barn. She recognized the skirt she'd worn yesterday.

The headline was slapped across the top in bright black letters: "Candy Arroyo Does It Again! Hot Encounter With Her Latest Squeeze At Charity Horse Show!"

What? Candy Arroyo? The actress? Janine squinted, looked at the picture again. The woman's face was turned toward the camera, a look of utter ecstasy on her face.

It *was* Candy Arroyo! That picture wasn't her and Del at all, now that she looked closer at it. She flipped through the magazine until she found the spread. More pictures. Of Candy, and her latest boyfriend. Both dressed very similarly to what she and Del had worn yesterday. So the pictures of Del and her could even be included in this spread, though she didn't think so. Had someone else scooped the photographer who'd taken the photos of her and Del with even clearer pictures showing Candy's face?

Shock made goose bumps stand up on her skin. Then a giddy, melty feeling warmed her all over, followed by a huge kick of regret as she realized what had been done on her behalf.

She so didn't deserve this.

Dear God. This whole thing had been a setup. To shove the photos of Del and her out of the limelight.

And she knew who'd done it.

Trust me.

Del had asked her to. And she hadn't.

Now she really did feel sick. Tears welled and spilled down her cheeks. She gripped the steering wheel, wanting to break down and sob.

You idiot. She slapped at the steering wheel, welcoming the sharp pain in her hands. She'd been so set on doing this on her own, to play the martyr and take her punishment instead of working with Del on a solution.

He'd solved the problem without her. He'd fixed it, just as he said he would. And she'd walked away from him. After insulting him, of course.

She didn't deserve a second chance with him, wouldn't blame him if he refused to talk to her.

But she was damn sure going to his house right now and beg his forgiveness.

He'd just saved her ass, her career, her company, even after all she'd said to him. But why? Why would he have done that for her, when he could have just walked away, blown her off as a rich bitch princess who couldn't handle the pressure?

She started the car and drove, swiping away the tears.

It was time for her to grow up, to stop worrying what everyone else thought, or might think. She'd been having a wonderful time with Del, until she'd ruined it. No one else had turned this into a disaster, had put a wedge between them.

She had.

Heart in her throat, she pulled into his driveway and shut off the engine, pocketed her keys and walked up to his front door. God, she hoped he was home. And that he was alone. She rang the doorbell, feeling dizzy and sick to her stomach, praying that he would at least give her a chance to apologize before slamming the door in her face.

He answered the door wearing shorts, no shirt, his hair a mess, a day's growth of beard on his face. He leaned against the doorway, obviously waiting for her to speak.

"Good morning."

"Mornin'," he said, his face giving nothing away. No emotion, no sense of whether he was happy to see her, or unhappy she'd showed up at his door.

Nothing. She, who had given speeches in front of thousands, couldn't find the words to apologize to the man she loved.

Say something, moron! "Can I come in?"

He tilted his head. "You didn't bring breakfast with you."

At least he was speaking to her, hadn't shut the door in her face. "Sorry. It was an impulse drive."

He shrugged. "That's okay." He stepped aside and she walked in, wringing her hands and feeling a surge of hope. She was nervous, didn't know what to say to him. She turned as soon as he shut the door. "I'm an ass."

He arched a brow. "You are?"

"Yes, and you know it. I'm so sorry."

His lips curled upward in a hint of a smile. "I take it you've seen the tabloids."

She nodded. "I should have trusted you."

He led her into his living room. "Yeah, you should have. I told you I'd take care of it."

"I know. I was in shock. I didn't think there was any way out." She slid onto the couch. "It's not a valid excuse. I'm so sorry, Del. I treated you so badly yesterday."

He shrugged. "Don't worry about it."

"Don't make excuses for me. I behaved like a shrew. And I should have believed you."

He sat next to her. Close to her. Then he picked up a strand of her hair, letting it slide through his fingers. She loved when he did that. It was so...possessive. Her heart began to race again, only this time the adrenaline rush wasn't from anxiety.

"I'd never leave you to face something like this alone, Janine. When we have sex together, we face the repercussions together."

"Is that how it is with…other women you've been with?"

"No. It's never been that way before. You're special."

"Why?" She threw it out there, needing to know the answer.

"Because I'm in love with you."

Her racing heart slammed on the brakes, crashing against her chest. "You love me?"

"Yes. *Je t'aime*, Janine."

Oh, God. In French, too. And that one she understood. She might fall over. "I love you, too."

He grinned. "Then you need to start trusting in me. I'll never let you dangle off the cliff alone."

She was crying now, and didn't care. Happiness had taken hold and wouldn't let go. "I told you I was an ass. And I worry too much about propriety and what's best for the foundation instead of what's best for me."

"And what is best for you?"

She crawled onto his lap. "You're what's best for me."

"Sounds like you're finally getting your priorities straight." He lifted her and carried her upstairs to his bedroom, depositing her on his bed. They both undressed, putting on a show for each other. Janine took the longest since she had more clothes on, which was fine with her. She stared down at his naked form, his cock erect and ready for her, and that emboldened her. She stood on the bed and stripped for Del, loving the way his gaze followed her every movement as she took off her clothing and tossed each piece to the floor. When she was naked, he crawled on the bed and swept his hands up her legs, her thighs, grasping her buttocks and pulling her toward him.

When he planted his mouth over her pussy, she cried out, shocked, yet oh so ready to feel his lips against her pussy. His mouth was hot, wet, his tongue rolling over the sensitive parts of her. The mattress was unsteady and she had to hold onto his head for support, because her legs were shaky and her body was trembling, too.

"Del." His tongue was magic, licking around her clit, diving into her pussy and making her crazy. She needed this release, desperate to let go of the tension that had held her in a tight vise the past day. And he was relentless in his quest, his fingers digging into the flesh of her buttocks and refusing to let her go. He licked her slow and easy, and she watched.

God, she loved watching. It heightened her senses, made everything she felt so much stronger. Seeing Del's tongue licking around her clit, and being able to feel the sensations, made her want more. And more. She tilted her hips, fisted his hair and dragged her swollen flesh over his tongue.

She came, bursting with pleasure as she shuddered against his rolling tongue and lips, warm cream spilling from her. Del held her tight against his face and slid his tongue inside her pussy to capture every drop.

Janine collapsed onto the bed and Del crawled up her body, kissing her stomach, her ribs, lingering at her breasts to plant kisses on her nipples, licking and sucking them until they stood high and wet and hard. She shivered as he covered her with his big body.

"Are you cold?" He looked down at her, his lips glistening with her juices.

She shook her head. "No. I'm hot."

He nudged her legs apart and flexed forward, his cockhead resting at the entrance to her pussy. "Don't I know it."

She lifted her head, kissed him, rimming his lips with her tongue before settling back down on the bed. "I love you, Del."

"I love you, too." He surged forward, his cock sliding easily inside her.

She wrapped her legs around him and welcomed him home, lifting her hips to meet every slow thrust of his cock. This was magic, this slow lovemaking in the darkened room. They didn't have the drapes open, no one could see them. It was just the two of them, alone, sharing their love, sharing kisses, murmuring soft words. His hands moved along her ribs, her hips, then back up again to smooth along her breasts. He touched her everywhere, spoke to her in a mixture of English and French, and her mind and body filled with love.

It was unhurried, emotional, and when she came, she sighed out his name and held tight as he groaned and spilled inside her with a shudder. Del rolled to his side and took her with him, his lips slanting across hers in a kiss that spoke of passion and tenderness.

Wrapped up in his arms was total bliss. "I don't think I ever want to leave this position."

He caressed her back. "You don't have to. We have all day."

She sighed. "So how did you do it?"

"With Candy?" He grinned. "She frequents Sneak Peek. A total exhibitionist, and she loves publicity. It was easy. I suggested and she went for it. We took pictures and made sure the tabloids got hold of them. I just made sure she and her guy wore the same clothes we had on yesterday."

She wasn't even going to ask how they managed to get the same clothing. Del was amazing.

"You're right. I should have trusted you to take care of it. I'll never forget that again."

He leaned in and kissed her, softly, and with a promise of so much more. "I'll never let you."

"I've done this alone for a long time, Del. My entire life, and especially since my father died."

"You don't have to be alone anymore. You have me."

"I've never had anyone before." It was frightening, exhilarating, daunting. "And you're...a handful."

He took her wrist and pulled her hand down to his already hardening cock. "I'll take that as a compliment."

She laughed.

"We've only scratched the surface, baby. There's so much we still have to explore together. Remember, you must live to enjoy life."

She squeezed his cock, stroked it, and felt life surging within her hand.

With Del, she intended to really begin to live her life, as she'd never lived it before. And she was going to stop looking over her shoulder to see if anyone was watching. Because she just didn't care anymore. Not as long as she had Del by her side.

"I'll trust you to show me all the ways there are to enjoy life," she said, then leaned in and kissed him.

About the Author

To learn more about Jaci Burton, please visit www.jaciburton.com. Send an email to Jaci Burton at jaci@jaciburton.com or join her Yahoo! group at http://groups.yahoo.com/group/jaciburtonsparadise to join in the fun with other readers as well as her newsletter at http://groups.yahoo.com/group/jaciburtonjournal for updates about future releases.

Look for these titles by
Jaci Burton

Now Available:

Rescue Me
Nothing Personal
Unwrapped
Dare to Love
Unraveled

It was nothing personal, just a business arrangement.

Nothing Personal
© *2007 Jaci Burton*

Ryan McKay is a multi-millionaire with a problem. He needs a bride to fulfill the terms of his grandfather's will. Unfortunately, the one he chose just bailed on him and he's hours away from losing his company. Enter Faith Lewis—his demure, devoted assistant. Ryan convinces Faith to step in and marry him, assuring her their marriage is merely a business deal. Ryan is certain he can keep this strictly impersonal. After all, he's the product of a loveless marriage and for years has sealed his own heart in an icy stone. Despite Faith's warmth, compassion and allure, he's convinced he's immune to her charms.

Faith will do anything for her boss, but—marry him? The shy virgin sees herself as plain and unattractive, a product of a bitter mother who drummed into her head that she wasn't worthy of a man's love. But she agrees to help Ryan fulfill the terms of his grandfather's will, hoping she doesn't lose her heart to him in the process.

But love rarely listens to logic, and what follows is anything but business.

Available now in ebook and print from Samhain Publishing.

By night, he becomes a mysterious stranger devoted only to her pleasure…and discovers she's hiding a naughty little secret.

Naughty Little Secret
© 2006 Shelley Bradley

After divorcing her never-home husband, Lauren Southall plucked up her courage, dusted off her power suits, and returned to corporate life. Two years later, there's just one six-foot three, testosterone-packed problem: her ex-husband's good friend and her current boss, Noah Reeves. Lauren aches for him. No other man will do. But she can't possibly measure up to the silicone-packed professional cheerleaders he dates. So she hides her desire behind a professional persona and fantasizes.

For ten years, Noah Reeves has waited to make Lauren his. Once her divorce was final, he tracked down and hired the brilliant, dedicated woman. But when he's with her, it isn't spreadsheets and profit margins on his brain. Problem is, she's never seen him as anything but her ex-husband's pal. Now that she's finally a free woman and with him 40+ hours a week, well… he'd love to persuade her to throw in her nights and weekends.

Noah decides to romance her by day. By night, he becomes a mysterious stranger devoted only to her pleasure…and discovers she's hiding a naughty little secret of her own.

Available now in ebook and print from Samhain Publishing.

Don't get mad...get sexy!

The Reinvention of Chastity
© *2007 Eve Vaughn*

Plain Jane paralegal Chastity Bryant has had a raving crush on her boss Sebastian Rossi since meeting him. Always willing to jump at his beck and call, Chastity's world comes crashing in on her one morning when she overhears him laughing about her less than exciting life. To top it off, he freely admits that he's used her crush to his advantage!

After a pep talk from her friends, they devise a plan to teach the arrogant Sebastian a lesson. Armed with a new look and a new attitude, Chastity sets out to seduce her hunky boss and bring him to his knees.

Sebastian Rossi has always been able to depend on two things in life: his successful law practice and his dependable employee, Chastity. But his whole world is turned upside down when she walks into his office looking like she just stepped off the cover of a magazine. Now, all he can think about is her. He doesn't know what brought about the change, but one thing is certain, he'll stop at nothing to possess her.

Things are going according to plan for Chastity, but the only thing she hadn't counted on was falling in love.

Available now in ebook and print from Samhain Publishing.

GET IT NOW

MyBookStoreAndMore.com

GREAT EBOOKS, GREAT DEALS . . . AND MORE!

Don't wait to run to the bookstore down the street, or
waste time shopping online at one of the "big boys." Now,
all your favorite Samhain authors are all in one place—at
MyBookStoreAndMore.com. Stop by today and discover
great deals on Samhain—and a whole lot more!

Samhain
Publishing
LTD

WWW.SAMHAINPUBLISHING.COM